WICKED DREAMS

AN IVY MORGAN MYSTERY BOOK TWO

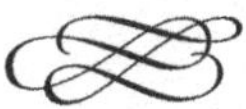

LILY HARPER HART

HARPERHART PUBLICATIONS

❀ Created with Vellum

ONE

Jack Harker's smile was one of those things that made Ivy Morgan's heart go pitter-patter at odd times.

This was one of those times.

"You look pretty, honey," Jack said, reaching over to brush her dark hair, which was shot through with bright streaks of pink, away from her face.

"Oh, this old thing," Ivy teased, glancing down at her maxi skirt and tank top. She owned her own plant nursery, so her wardrobe choices were all her own. She didn't have a work uniform, but if she did, this was the closest thing to it. Almost everything in her closet resembled her current ensemble.

At five-foot-seven, Ivy was relatively tall for a woman. Jack still towered over her, his body a protective mass of muscle and strength that often tilted her over into schmaltzy fantasies. It was a recent development, and one she wasn't particularly proud of. That didn't stop her from doing it, though.

Ivy lifted her hand and touched Jack's cheek, rubbing her thumb over his strong jaw. "You're pretty, too."

"Oh, honey, I'm not pretty," Jack said, cupping her hand with his and holding it in place. "Men aren't pretty. I'm manly and handsome. Get it right."

One of the things Ivy liked most about Jack was that he wasn't too serious. As a police officer, he was dedicated to his job – and he had a haunted past that he didn't want to talk about – but when interacting with her, he was often playful and always charming.

He was also bossy, but since that was a trait they shared, Ivy could live with it. They bossed each other around, argued incessantly, and fought off enough sexual tension to fill a stadium.

They were just friends, she reminded herself. Jack was upfront with her when they met. He wasn't looking for a relationship. Of course, that didn't mean he could stay away from her. So far he'd helped her uncover a murderer, played a rousing game of horse on the basketball court (which he lost), and found several reasons to stop in at Morgan's Nursery for landscaping ideas related to an ongoing restoration project at his new house. Every interaction was fun and sexually charged. They'd also been chaste.

She wasn't looking for a relationship either. Well, that was the mantra she repeated over and over in her head on a daily basis. She was a witch, after all. She was odd, loudmouthed, obsessive, and often irrational. She wanted to live her life in a specific way, and if people didn't understand that, she didn't have time for them.

A bonafide city boy, Jack never flinched at the whispers and stares that followed Ivy around town. He didn't care that she identified as a spiritual naturalist. He didn't care that she preferred to lose herself in books rather than strutting around Shadow Lake, a blink-and-you'll-miss-it tiny hamlet in northern Lower Michigan, like she was some sort of modern fashion plate. He even embraced her belief in magic without making fun of her or casting sidelong glances when he thought she wasn't looking.

He was perfect in almost every way – and yet they were still treading water and just "hanging out" when the mood struck. Jack couldn't get over his past, and Ivy was too frightened to look toward a future.

So how did they end up here?

"The sun is setting," Jack said, tightening his grip on Ivy's hand and pointing toward the top of the tree line. The sky looked like it was on fire.

"The sun set four hours ago," Ivy said, sighing. "We're in a dream."

"You know you're in a dream?" Jack asked, lifting a dark eyebrow.

"Don't you?"

"No," Jack said. "I think it must be your dream. I'm just here to be eye candy. That must be my job in your subconscious."

Ivy snickered. "You're good at your job."

"I am," Jack agreed. He glanced down at her, his molten chocolate eyes serious as they studied her expressive face. "I wish you were this … settled … when you're awake. I like you this way."

"What way is that?" Ivy asked.

"Relaxed."

"I'm relaxed in real life," Ivy scoffed. "You just think I'm not because whenever we're around each other, I keep imagining you naked and it makes me snarky."

Jack barked out a coarse laugh. "I can't believe you admitted that. Just for the record, though, you're not fooling anyone. I know what you're thinking when you look at me."

"How?"

"Because I'm thinking the same thing," Jack said.

"Well, I guess it's good this is a dream," Ivy said, resting her head against his shoulder and staring out at the setting sun. "I can say whatever I want."

"You can say whatever crosses that weird little mind of yours when you're awake, too," Jack said, his hand drifting up and enveloping her back so he could hold her close. "I like it when you say whatever you want. Most of the time, it's funny."

"Maybe I should be a comedian."

"You can be the wickedest comedian witch in the Midwest," Jack teased.

"I think you're making fun of me," Ivy said, jutting her lower lip out.

"I would never make fun of you," Jack said, cupping her head and holding it still so he could gaze into her eyes.

"You always make fun of me," Ivy countered, her mouth running dry due to the proximity of Jack's beckoning lips. "I … um … what are you doing?"

"It's a dream, Ivy," Jack said, lowering his mouth to hers. "I can do whatever I want."

IVY BOLTED UPRIGHT in her bed, her heart pounding and her stomach rolling as the filmy headiness of the fantasy landscape slid aside to make way for the early morning sun wafting through her bedroom curtains.

It was a dream. She knew that while she was having it, and yet it was still disappointing to wake up right when she was getting to the good part.

The black cat on the bed next to her opened one eye and glared, annoyed to have his morning slumber so rudely interrupted. Ivy stroked his soft fur. "I'm sorry I woke you, Nicodemus."

If cats could roll their eyes, Ivy was sure that's what Nicodemus was doing. It was almost as if he knew what she'd been dreaming about.

"Don't look at me like that," Ivy said. "I'm allowed to dream. I still don't want a relationship. Jack doesn't want one either. We're just … friends."

Nicodemus didn't look like he believed her.

"We are. Stop looking at me like that." Ivy climbed out of the bed, leaving the cat to his judgmental morning sojourn, and padded toward the shower. She was already up – even though her alarm clock wasn't set to go off for another half hour – and she figured now was as good of a time as any to start her day. Spring was in full swing in Shadow Lake, and that meant the nursery would be bustling with garden enthusiasts. A steady clientele was exactly what Ivy needed to put her dreams of Jack Harker where they belonged: in the back of her mind.

Now she just had to convince her heart to agree with her mind.

"I NEED a tree that takes zero work." Charlotte Jones was a Shadow Lake lifer. She'd been born in the small hamlet forty years before, and she had every intention of dying there. She'd recently built her dream house with her husband, and now they were ready for the landscaping step.

"Most trees don't take a lot of work after the first few weeks," Ivy said. "What kind of tree do you want?"

"One that doesn't take any work," Charlotte said.

Ivy pursed her lips. She'd learned a long time ago that the customer was always right, even when they didn't give her much to go on. "Okay," she said, racking her brain. "What do you want the tree to represent?"

"I have an open spot in the front of my lawn and it's bugging me," Charlotte said. "I want a tree to put there so it doesn't bug me."

Well, that was helpful, Ivy internally snarked. "Do you want a pine tree?"

"Those are ugly."

"How about a maple or oak?"

Charlotte furrowed her brow. "Those shed leaves in the fall, right?"

Ivy nodded.

"That's work," Charlotte said.

Well, at least they were narrowing down the choices. "How about a flowering tree?" Ivy suggested. "There's a flowering crabapple that is absolutely beautiful, and when the blooms drop you can just mow right over them."

"Sold," Charlotte said. "That sounds great."

Ivy smiled. "I don't have any out on the lot," she said. "I have some in the greenhouse. Give me a few minutes and I can bring one up. How big do you want it to be?"

"Which size is the easiest to plant?"

Ivy figured she should've expected that question. "I'm going to recommend the larger tree," she said. "It's more expensive, but it's also hardier. It's going to take a little more work to plant, but once you have it in the ground, other than watering it regularly the first few weeks, it should be effortless."

"That sounds great," Charlotte said. "My husband is responsible for planting it. I'm just responsible for picking it out. He said, since I insist on shopping for everything, I had to shop for this, too."

Ivy had a feeling Charlotte's dream house wasn't leading to a dream marriage, but she didn't say that out loud. "I'll go and get the tree."

"Take your time," Charlotte said. "I need to pick out a few other things."

"I'll put it up by the register," Ivy said. "I'll put your name on it. Just tell Dad it's yours when you're checking out."

"Thanks, Ivy," Charlotte said. "You're a lifesaver."

After chatting up a few more customers, Ivy stopped near the register long enough to tell her father, Michael, she was going to be in the greenhouse for a few minutes so he could be available to answer client questions if they popped up.

Since he was her silent partner in the business and he loved horticulture, Ivy knew it wouldn't be too much of a hardship.

"Hey, little missy," Michael said, smiling at his daughter as she approached. "How are you today? No hug for your dear, old dad?"

Ivy stepped into his warm embrace, returning the gesture with a tight squeeze, and then took a step back. Her parents were part-timers in Shadow Lake. They spent the winter months in Florida to get away from the cold and snow, and the summer months in Michigan. They'd only been home a few weeks, and while Ivy loved them, she was already starting to chafe under their constant presence.

"Better?" she asked, cocking an eyebrow.

"My life is always better when I have a little Ivy in it," Michael teased. "What's going on?"

"I have to run back to the greenhouse," Ivy said. "Charlotte Jones needs a crabapple tree. I need you to keep an eye on everything up here."

"I aim to please," Michael said, mock saluting. "That's not what I was getting at, though."

Ivy furrowed her brow. "What were you getting at?"

"How is your love life?"

Ivy internally groaned, rolling her eyes as she regarded him with a serious expression. "Non-existent."

"Don't lie to your father," Michael chided. "When you do that a fairy dies."

"That's what you told me when I was eight and you caught me trying to hide that kitten in my bedroom," Ivy said. "I believed it then. I'm far too savvy to believe it now."

"You believe it a little bit," Michael replied, nonplussed.

The sad thing is, he was right. "Fine," Ivy said, blowing out a sigh. "I still don't have a love life, though."

"What about Jack?"

"What about him?"

"Harry Morton told me he saw you two playing basketball up at the high school last week," Michael said, not missing a beat.

"How does that constitute me having a love life?"

"He said you two were laughing and ... flirting."

"He saw that from where, his perch in the tree where he was spying on us?" Ivy was irritated. She was used to people gossiping about her. She didn't like the idea of her time with Jack being monitored, though. It made her uncomfortable.

"People are on couple watch, Ivy," Michael said, unruffled. "Everyone knows you and Jack are circling each other like sharks about to strike."

"*Shark Week* isn't until August," Ivy said. "How can you possibly pull that analogy out of your butt in May?"

"Nice," Michael said, smirking. "Tell me about Jack."

"There's nothing to tell about Jack," Ivy said. "How many times do I have to tell you that?"

"Just until you believe it," Michael said.

Ivy rolled her eyes. "I'm going to the greenhouse."

"That's fine," Michael said, refusing to let his only daughter bait him. "This conversation will be available to revisit at any time."

"Great," Ivy said, turning on her heel and stalking toward the greenhouse at the edge of the property. "I can't wait."

"I love you, too," Michael called to her back before focusing on a customer.

Ivy's agitation grew with every step. She knew her father was trying to be supportive, but everyone watching her made her sick to her stomach. She wanted to live her life on her terms – not everyone else's.

Ivy let herself into the greenhouse, taking her time to scan up and down the rows as she tried to remember where the crabapples were located. After a few moments, she remembered they were in the back corner.

Upon finding them, she studied her options for a few minutes before selecting one of the biggest ones she had to offer. Since Charlotte wasn't planting it, Ivy figured she would be thrilled about giving her husband more work.

Ivy had the tree in her arms and escape on her mind when she heard something shuffle in the area behind her. She shifted, narrowing her eyes so she could stare into the corner behind some germinating hydrangeas. She'd just about convinced herself she imagined it when she saw a hint of movement.

She peered closer, her heart inadvertently flipping when she caught sight of a hint of dirty blonde hair and a pair of terrified green eyes. It was a girl … a teenage one, if Ivy was right with her initial scan.

Ivy opened her mouth to speak, thinking a parent had probably brought the girl to the nursery and she'd just gotten lost, when the girl realized she'd been discovered. She opened her mouth, too … and screamed.

TWO

"I called Brian Nixon," Michael said, moving up to Ivy's side as she leaned against the greenhouse doorframe. "He's on his way."

Brian Nixon was a police detective with the Shadow Lake Police Department – and Jack's partner. Ivy couldn't focus on Jack's impending arrival, though. She had a few other things on her mind.

After screaming bloody murder, the girl curled up into a small ball and pressed her back to the wall in the far corner of the greenhouse. Ivy tried to talk to and touch her, but that only garnered more screaming. Finally, the worried woman moved to the door so she could watch without terrifying her guest.

"She's got bruises all over her arms," Ivy said, her voice low. "She's filthy, too."

Michael swallowed hard as he patted Ivy's shoulder. He knew what she was thinking. It was the exact same thing worrying him. "How long do you think she's been in there?"

"I have no idea," Ivy said. "I was in the greenhouse yesterday, but only to grab a couple of pots close to the door. She could've been in here then ... which freaks me out."

"It's okay, kid," Michael said. "You couldn't have known. I was in here yesterday, too."

"Someone hurt her, Dad," Ivy said. "She's ... traumatized."

"It's going to be okay, Ivy," Michael said. "You found her. The police are on their way. They'll know exactly what to do."

Ivy hoped that was true. Something told her the road to finding out who this girl was – and what happened to her – was going to be a bumpy one.

"WELL, CRAP," Brian said, scurrying back outside the greenhouse and fixing Ivy with a conflicted look. "She won't let me get close to her."

"Join the club," Michael said. "We've both tried, too."

Jack shifted uncomfortably, proximity to Ivy causing his heart rate to speed up while he tried to focus on the task at hand. "Maybe I should try."

"No," Ivy said, immediately shaking her head.

"Why not? I might be able to get through to her."

"I know you mean well, but she's in shock or something," Ivy said. "You're too big. You're going to scare her."

"I'm too big?" Jack widened his eyes, incredulous.

"You know what I mean," Ivy said. "You're all muscles and broad shoulders. She's scared and you're physically intimidating. Plus, you're wearing a red shirt and that can be taken as antagonistic to some people."

"Thanks for the fashion critique, honey," Jack said, using the affectionate nickname he'd adopted a few weeks before. She'd used it first without thinking. He'd opted to start using it to irritate her. Now he kind of liked it, and it slipped out even when he didn't want it to. They really were in a weird spot in their relationship, and both of them were struggling to maintain even footing. Finding a disheveled and possibly abused teenage girl in the greenhouse wasn't going to help the situation.

"Well, *honey*, you're going to make her scream if you go in there, and that's what we're trying to avoid," Ivy said.

Michael and Brian exchanged a look, one that wasn't lost on Jack and Ivy. They were amused by the banter, enjoying the show even though bigger issues were weighing down on them.

"What do you suggest?" Jack asked, his hands landing on his narrow hips as he regarded Ivy. She really was aggravating … and hot … and she smelled delightful. He had no idea what the scent was, but it was going straight to his head.

"I don't know," Ivy replied primly. "I … ." She stuck her head back in the room for a moment, her eyes finding the shaking girl in the corner. "Okay, I have a plan."

"I can't wait to hear this," Jack said.

Ivy ignored him. "Dad, I need you to go back to my house," she said. "There's some egg salad in the refrigerator. Make two sandwiches and grab the bag of broccoli in the bottom drawer. Bring a couple of bottles of water, too. She's probably thirsty."

"You're going to bribe her with food?" Jack asked.

"I'll be back in a few minutes," Michael said, not bothering to argue with Ivy's order.

"I think I need to call for some paramedics," Brian said. "She looks … rough."

"Call Samantha Hobbes," Ivy suggested.

"Why her?"

"She's a woman."

"Ivy, I know what you're thinking," Brian said. "I'm not ruling that out. We don't know that she's been hurt *that* way, though. Not yet."

"I'm taking every precaution," Ivy said. "Trust me. I hope she hasn't been hurt that way. It's going to make me really sad if it's true … but we have to be careful either way."

"Okay," Brian said, giving in. "I'm going to let you take the lead – but only because I don't know what else to do."

"Every man in my life should always take that approach where I'm concerned," Ivy sniffed.

Jack pursed his lips. "I agree," he said after a moment. "I think we should start carrying you around on our shoulders and exalt your virtue and loveliness every chance we get."

Ivy made a face. "You're going to owe me a big apology when I'm right on this."

"I'm looking forward to it, honey."

IVY GRIPPED the sandwich plate in her hand and pressed the bottles of water to her chest as she shuffled toward the back corner of the greenhouse twenty minutes later. She knew Brian – and more importantly, Jack – watched her from the doorway. She didn't want to fail, and sadly, it wasn't just because she wanted to help the girl. She also wanted to be right.

Ivy lowered herself to a sitting position and rested the plate and bottles of water on the ground. She carefully pushed them over until they were within reaching distance for the girl, and then she pushed herself back until she was close enough to watch her but far away enough to appear unthreatening.

"You should eat something," Ivy said, keeping her voice soft. "It's egg salad and broccoli. I don't have a lot of junk food around my house. I'm sorry."

The girl shifted her position, pushing herself upright as her eyes darted between Ivy and the plate.

"I promise it's good," Ivy said.

Either the girl was opting to trust her – or she was just that hungry – because she grabbed the sandwich and shoved it into her mouth without uttering a word. Ivy had never seen anyone inhale a sandwich that fast, and she was relieved when the girl approached the second sandwich with tepid moderation.

"Have some water," Ivy prodded.

The girl suspiciously took the water, casting one more look at Ivy before opening and guzzling it. She didn't put the water bottle down until it was empty, and then she immediately reached for the second bottle.

Ivy's heart rolled painfully. The girl was starving and dehydrated. Upon closer inspection, the bruises on her arms were darker and more numerous than Ivy realized. She had a feeling that they weren't relegated to just her arms either.

"My name is Ivy. This is my greenhouse. I own the whole nursery, actually. My house is just through the woods, too."

The girl didn't respond, but her thoughtful eyes were focused on Ivy as she reached for the broccoli and started munching.

"I grew up here," Ivy continued. "This is a very special place. I'm betting that's why you were drawn here."

There was still no answer. Ivy decided to do what came naturally: talk.

"Are you from around here? I'll bet you're from close by," she said. "Did you have to walk here? Do you want more to eat? Do you want to come out and let me get a better look at you?"

This went on … and on … and on.

"WE HAVE TO DO SOMETHING," Jack said, leaning his head against the wall of the greenhouse and turning his attention to Michael and Brian. "She's floundering in there."

"She's not floundering," Michael argued. "She's trying to build a rapport."

"She just talking … and talking … and talking," Jack said. "The girl isn't talking back."

"She's not screaming either," Brian said. "Give Ivy a little time. She might surprise you with how good she is with people."

"I didn't say she wasn't good with people."

"You were insinuating it," Michael said, shooting him a look. "I'll have you know, my daughter is good at whatever she does. No, I take that back. She's great at whatever she does. You should have a little faith in her."

Jack was taken aback. "I didn't say I didn't have faith in her. I … she's not getting anywhere, though."

"She got her to eat without screaming," Brian said. "That's more than you or I could've accomplished."

"You don't know that," Jack said. "I'm very charming. I'm also easy to talk to."

"That must be why you and Ivy are always sniping at one another," Brian said drily.

"That's the sexual tension," Michael said.

Jack's cheeks colored. He was well aware that the town was talking about his flirtation with Ivy. He could deal with that. He was new to town. He didn't know most of the people who lived there, so he didn't care what they thought. For Ivy's father to point it out, though, was something else entirely. "I … ."

"Oh, look how cute he is," Brian said, smirking. "You've completely thrown him off his game."

Jack recovered quickly. "I am not off my game. Nothing throws me off my game. I'm a professional."

"I heard Ivy beat you at basketball last week," Brian said.

"She didn't beat me," Jack said. "She … played me. She didn't tell me she could've tried out for the WNBA and made it on half of the teams before we started."

"She's always been a good athlete," Michael said, chuckling. "She's not that good, though."

"She had home court advantage," Jack grumbled. "We're having a rematch now that I know what I'm up against. I won't let her win again."

"Wait," Brian said, holding up his hand. "Did you lose because she's good enough to be in the WNBA, she had home court advantage, or you let her win? Those are three different things."

"I … let it go," Jack sputtered. "We have more important things to focus on."

"We do," Brian agreed, grinning despite himself. "We have to focus on the basketball star and the fact that she doesn't like to lose any more than you do. Trust me. She's going to find a way to win in this situation, too."

"I'm not sure there's going to be any way to win this situation," Jack said, sobering. "This is going to be bad no matter what."

. . .

"CAN'T YOU PLEASE SAY SOMETHING?" Ivy asked. "I'm not asking for a full sentence. Just say one word. Tell me to shut up if you want to. I can take it."

The girl tilted her head to the side, her dirty blonde hair dipping low on her shoulders as she regarded Ivy.

"Please," Ivy prodded.

"I'm still hungry."

The words took Ivy by surprise and yet caused her heart to soar at the same time. While the girl wasn't opening up about her ordeal, or even saying her name, she also wasn't closing herself off to the possibility of Ivy helping her.

"I can deal with that," Ivy said. "I have a lot more food back at the house. If you don't like any of it, I'm betting I can get something delivered that you will like."

"I . . . ." The girl broke off, biting her lower lip uncertainly.

"I'm not going to pressure you," Ivy said. "I just want you to stand up and walk with me."

"Can't you just bring the food out here?"

"No," Ivy said, shaking her head. "This isn't a place for food. It will draw scavengers. I can take you out of here, though. I can help you get cleaned up. I can feed you as much as you want to eat. You have to trust me, though."

The girl shrank back slightly.

"I promise you can trust me," Ivy said, extending her hand. "I won't hurt you. I won't let anyone hurt you. I'm meaner than I look in case you're worried about someone coming to look for you here. I won't let anyone touch you."

The girl studied Ivy's hand for a moment and Ivy's heart stuttered when she finally reached out and took it. Ivy kept her smile in place as she helped the girl to her feet and started to lead her out of the greenhouse.

It wasn't much. It wasn't answers. It wasn't a solution. It wasn't a happily ever after. It was something, though, and for now Ivy was more than willing to take it.

THREE

"Absolutely not," Jack said, gritting his teeth as he leaned against Ivy's counter.

After leading the girl to her house – bypassing the helpful paramedic with an apologetic smile – and promising to find something for her to eat while she was in the bathroom taking a shower, Ivy informed Brian and Jack that she was keeping the girl until she felt safe enough to talk.

Brian was blasé about the announcement while Jack was bitterly against it. Ivy was expecting both reactions.

"Why not?" Ivy crossed her arms over her chest obstinately.

"Because I said so," Jack replied.

"She's going to be comfortable here," Ivy said. "It will be me and her. There won't be anyone to scare her. If it's just the two of us I might be able to get her to open up. How can that possibly be a bad idea?"

Jack made a face. "That's not how things work in situations like this," he said. "We have to call the state. They have people – counselors even – who are trained to deal with things like this. The girl has obviously been abused. You can't fix that for her."

"I didn't say I could fix it."

Jack sucked in a long, calming breath. Flying off the handle wasn't going to accomplish anything. All it would do was get Ivy's hackles up – and no one wanted that. "I know you want to help her," he said, keeping his voice low. "I commend you for it. Just because she was found on your property, though, that doesn't mean she's your responsibility."

"I don't like the way you're talking down to me," Ivy said, her blue eyes narrowing. "I'm not a child."

"I didn't say you were a child," Jack said. "When did I say you were a child?"

"You were talking to me like I'm two and I want a cookie but I've hit my sugar limit for the day," Ivy said.

"I was not."

"You were, too."

"I was not."

"You were, too."

They both turned to Brian expectantly. He seemed surprised to be included in the conversation. "Oh, don't look at me," he said. "I was just wondering where the playground moderator was to break you two up."

"See," Jack said triumphantly.

"I was talking to you, too," Brian said, nonplussed.

"See," Ivy said, sticking her tongue out.

The gesture was supposed to irritate Jack – and it did – but it also turned him on. He could think of a few other things he wanted to do with that tongue, like rub it against his own. *Oh, man, he was losing it.* There could be no other explanation. He had to try a different tactic. "Ivy, even if we wanted to let her stay here with you, we can't," Jack said. "She needs a social worker. Tell her, Brian."

Brian cleared his throat as he shifted uncomfortably. "I think she should stay here."

"What?" Jack's eyebrows nearly flew off his forehead as he turned on his partner.

"I'm not suggesting she move in and become Ivy's ward or

anything," Brian said, lifting his hands to hold off Jack's fury. "I'm suggesting she spend the night."

"How is that going to help?" Jack asked, refusing to surrender even though he was outnumbered.

"It's going to give the girl a chance to catch her breath in an unthreatening atmosphere," Brian said. "If Ivy can get her to talk, we might be able to find some answers. We might be able to help her."

"Ivy isn't trained to handle anything like this," Jack countered.

"You don't have to be trained to be a good sounding board," Brian said. "I'm not asking you to go against your instincts. I'm asking you to give Ivy one night and then we'll regroup and make a decision tomorrow."

"I … ." Jack pinched the bridge of his nose and shifted his gaze to Ivy. He expected her to be aggressive and vehement. Instead, he found her eyes bright and pleading. He couldn't say no, even if he wanted to. "Okay."

"Really?" Ivy looked surprised.

"Really," Jack said, his voice softening. "Be careful, Ivy. She's been through something. I know you want to help and I believe you can. You can't fix everything in that girl's life, though. It's not possible. Promise me you're not going to … go overboard."

"I promise," Ivy said, instinctively throwing her arms around his neck and offering him a grateful hug.

Jack was surprised by the gesture, and he initially thought he should pull away from her, but she felt too good in his arms to ignore. He hugged her back, and when he met Brian's delighted smile from over her shoulder, he found he didn't care so much that his partner was saving up a bevy of things to tease him about later.

Once they separated, Ivy regained her senses quickly. "I'll call you if I find anything out," she said.

"Call me tomorrow morning regardless," Jack said. "We're going to have decisions to make no matter what happens tonight."

"Okay."

"I can't believe you're being this easy to deal with," Jack muttered.

"I promise I'll be good," Ivy said. "I know you warned me not to go overboard, but you should know, I never go overboard."

Jack didn't know her well, but he knew enough to know that was a blatant lie. "I just know I'm going to regret this."

"**WHERE** DID THE POLICEMEN GO?"

Ivy, who was sitting on the couch in the living room when the girl finally left the bathroom, lifted her head and smiled. "They left."

"I thought they wanted to arrest me."

"Why would they want to arrest you?" Ivy shifted over on the couch, clearing a spot for the girl should she want to sit, but she didn't force her. The yoga pants and T-shirt Ivy left for the teenager were big on her narrow hips, and now that she could see her figure in its entirety, it was clear she was malnourished. Her hipbones were protruding through the thin cotton fabric, and her elbows were knobby. Ivy had every intention of fixing that.

"I trespassed."

"You got turned around," Ivy corrected. "It's my property. It's only trespassing if I say it is. I say you got turned around. Don't worry about it."

"I … thank you."

"Don't mention it," Ivy said, forcing her face to remain neutral even as the dark bruises on the girl's arm caught her attention again. "I … can you sit over here with me? I'd like to take a look at those bruises."

"They're fine," the girl said, tilting her head to the side and studying Ivy's cottage. "Do you live here alone?"

"Yes."

"You're not married?"

"No."

"Do you have a boyfriend?"

Ivy chuckled. "No. Everyone keeps trying to find me one, though."

"The tall cop with the dark eyes? Is he the one who everyone wants you to be with?"

Ivy was surprised by the girl's question. She'd obviously been watching the situation as it progressed outside the greenhouse. She was intuitive … and smart. Ivy just hoped she could reach her on a personal level so she could get some insight into her as well.

"How did you know that?" Ivy asked.

"He looks at you in a funny way," the girl said. "You look at him the same way."

"I do not."

"You both do. You just don't do it at the same time. You only look at each other when you think the other isn't looking."

Ivy rolled her eyes. "Are you going to hop on the Ivy and Jack train, too?"

"Maybe," the girl said.

Ivy patted the couch. "Let me check your bruises."

"I'm fine."

"If you let me check your bruises, I'll tell you all about Jack," Ivy said. She wasn't above bribery. She knew it could be an effective measure when she really wanted something and she really wanted the girl to open up.

"Okay." The girl gave in and approached Ivy slowly. She was cautious in her movements, and Ivy knew why. She was used to people lashing out at her.

Once the girl was settled, Ivy carefully lifted her arms and studied them. After a few moments, she raised her eyes to the girl's. "I have some cream that will help these fade. It's just in the bathroom. I'm going to go get it."

The girl nodded.

When Ivy returned a few minutes later, she found Nicodemus rubbing himself against the girl's chest, purring as he encouraged her to stroke him. For her part, the girl seemed mesmerized by his green eyes and soft fur.

"That's Nicodemus."

"He's sweet."

"He's spoiled," Ivy countered, purposely keeping her approach slow and her movements exaggerated as she sat back down on the couch.

"How long have you had him?"

"I found him in a Dumpster in town five years ago," Ivy said. "Someone threw him in there when he was too young to fend for himself. I bottle-fed him for weeks. I was going to try and find a home for him, but I got too attached and I couldn't give him up when it was time."

"He's lucky you're the one who found him."

"I think we were both lucky," Ivy said, squeezing a dollop of cream into her hand and transferring it over to the girl's arm. "Do you want to tell me your name?"

The girl stiffened, causing Ivy to backtrack.

"You don't have to tell me your name," Ivy said. "If you don't want to tell me, that's perfectly okay. I do need something to call you, though. Do you have a favorite name?"

"You want me to make up a name for myself?"

"I want you to tell me what you want me to call you," Ivy clarified. "I would prefer your real name, but if you're not comfortable with that, I can call you whatever you want. I've always liked the name Iris. How about that?"

The girl wrinkled her nose. "Iris?"

"I like plant names," Ivy said, not missing a beat. "I can't tell you why. It might be because I work in a nursery. If you don't like Iris, though, there are a lot of other options. We could try Rose? No? Okay. How about Pansy? Lily?"

The girl shot down every suggestion with a shake of her head.

"Okay," Ivy said, giving up. "It's your turn to tell me what you want me to call you."

The girl licked her lips, shifting her gaze to the small fireplace at the edge of the room before glancing back at Ivy. "My name is Kelly Sisto."

Ivy wanted to crow, but she tempered her enthusiasm instead. "Kelly is a nice name."

"I like your name," Kelly said, smiling ruefully. "It … fits you."

"Most people agree," Ivy said, shifting her attention to Kelly's other arm.

"Are you an only child?"

"No. I have a brother. His name is Max. We grew up in this house together, though. It used to belong to my parents, but now it's mine."

"Did they die?"

It was pointed question, and Ivy couldn't help but think there was something more behind it. "No. They just moved to a house that wasn't so isolated. They're a little older now, and they spend their winters in Florida. They knew how much I loved this house, though, so they sold it to me a few years ago."

"That's nice," Kelly said. "I like your house. It's … homey."

"It is," Ivy said. "What is your house like?"

"I don't want to talk about that."

"Okay," Ivy said. "What do you want to talk about?"

"I … tell me about growing up in this house," Kelly said. "I'll bet it was magical."

Ivy decided the best way to get Kelly to open up was to do it herself. So, without a second thought, she delved into the story of her childhood, and she didn't stop until Kelly was done asking questions.

It took two hours, but Kelly was comfortable with Ivy by the time they were done. Just when Ivy was about to broach the subject of Kelly's past, though, the sound of a vehicle door slamming in the driveway caught her attention.

Kelly jumped to her feet, terror flitting across her face. "Who's here? Did he find me?"

Ivy raised her hand to soothe her. "No. I promise no one will get you here." She glanced out to the driveway, making a face when she saw who was striding up her front walk. "Don't worry. They're not here for you."

"Who is it?"

"Well, you wanted to know more about my family," Ivy said, smiling ruefully. "You're about to get your wish."

FOUR

"You can't come in."

Luna Morgan met her daughter's plaintive gaze with a blank one of her own. "What do you mean we can't come in?"

"I have a guest," Ivy said.

"Is he naked?" Max asked, wrinkling his nose.

"Who?"

"Your guest," Max said.

"It's not a man," Ivy said, rolling her eyes. "Get your mind out of the gutter."

"We know it's not a man," Luna said, patting Ivy's arm. "As much as we'd like it to be Jack, we ran into him downtown when we were heading into the diner for dinner. We know you kept the girl you found in the greenhouse."

"Jack has a big mouth," Ivy grumbled.

"He was worried," Max said. "As much as he likes to pretend he doesn't have feelings for you, he's already a goner. Brian was trying to cheer him up with pie, and Maisie was trying to cheer him up with her boobs, but he was fighting both of their efforts."

"I … ." Ivy broke off, narrowing her eyes. "What do you mean Maisie was trying to cheer him up with her boobs?"

In addition to being the town librarian, Maisie Washington was also Shadow Lake's resident harlot. She'd never met a single man she didn't want to seduce … and the marital status of her target didn't often stand in her way. She was willing to take on husbands, too.

Max smirked. "Don't worry. Jack doesn't want to see anyone's boobs but yours."

Michael cuffed his son. "Don't say things like that. She's your sister."

"She knows she has boobs," Max replied, nonplussed.

"Yes, and brothers aren't supposed to comment on them," Luna said. "They only do that in certain families, and we're not one of them."

Max's face colored. "That's not what I meant."

"We know," Michael said. "We like to embarrass you anyway." He turned to Ivy and lifted the bag he was carrying. "We brought food."

That was convenient since Kelly was still making noises about being hungry. Still … . "Thank you for the food," Ivy said, grabbing the bag. "I'll talk to you guys tomorrow."

"Don't you want to invite us in?" Luna prodded.

"No."

"Ivy," Michael said, keeping his voice low. "We're coming in."

"We promise not to be too loud," Luna said, putting her hand on Ivy's wrist and cutting her off before she could argue. "We just want to see her. We want to help you if we can. We're a family, and if you're taking this girl on as part of your family, that means she's part of our family, too."

"It's going to be okay," Max said. "I promise."

"Fine," Ivy said, cursing under her breath. "She's skittish, though. Her name is Kelly. She hasn't opened up about her past and she's not ready yet, so don't press her on it. She also seems scared of men, so Dad and Max, you need to give her a wide berth."

Everyone nodded solemnly.

"There will be no sudden movements," Ivy said. "There will be no wrestling. Max, I'm talking to you. No noogies. No putting anyone's head in your armpit. No wedgies."

"No offense, Ivy, but I haven't tried to give you a wedgie since you started wearing the same kind of underwear my dates did," Max said, making a face. "I'm scarred for life from that last one. Here I was thinking you were still playing with Barbie dolls and instead you were dressing like one. Ugh."

Ivy pinched the bridge of her nose. "Max, there will be no talking about anything like that either."

"Ivy, I've got it," Max said, shooting her a charming grin. "I promise to be on my best behavior. I won't do anything bad. I'm not an idiot."

As annoying as she found her brother, Ivy knew Max had a good heart. He would never go out of his way to purposely hurt someone. She felt guilty about suggesting otherwise. "Okay," she said. "We're just a normal family hanging out with greasy diner food and a runaway teenage girl."

Ivy knew that wasn't the truth, but she wasn't above deluding herself when the opportunity arose.

"DO YOU LIKE HAMBURGERS, KELLY?" Luna asked, unpacking the bag of goodies on the kitchen table and fixing the timid girl with a wide smile. "We got a little of everything because we didn't know what you would like."

"I'll ... eat anything," Kelly replied, her voice low and breathy. "You didn't have to get all of this food for me."

"We got it for everyone," Michael said, winking from his spot in the armchair at the edge of Ivy's living room. He'd taken Ivy's words to heart, sitting almost immediately and keeping his movements small. His normally booming voice was muted, but his words were kind and his eyes retained their infamous twinkle.

Max was another story. "Ivy is a vegetarian," he said, handing Kelly a container. "She only eats vegetables and crap. Don't get me wrong, she's an excellent cook, but she's never embraced the joys of eating a good steak."

Kelly hesitantly took the container from Max. "You're not a vegetarian?"

"We tried to indoctrinate him into the family vegetarian fold," Luna said. "He broke free when he was in elementary school, although he still pretended until he got into middle school."

"And I never looked back," Max said jovially. "Don't worry. If you like meat, I'll make sure to keep you in it while you're staying with Ivy. I would hate to think of you going without just because Ivy eats carrots instead of jerky."

Kelly shifted her green eyes to Ivy worriedly. "I don't have to eat meat."

"Go ahead," Ivy said. "It's fine. I'm not one of those vegetarians who tells everyone else what to eat. I only care about what I eat."

"She's lying," Max whispered. "She tried to convince me that soy bacon was the same as regular bacon last week. Just a hint: It's not."

Kelly pressed her lips together, her eyes wide as she took in Max at his charming best. Ivy couldn't be sure, but she thought she saw a hint of a crush forming there. If that was the case, and Kelly could so easily accept him in her presence, Ivy was hopeful her initial fears were wrong. Kelly had clearly been abused, but if that abuse stopped short of being sexual, she would be forever thankful.

"I'll have you know that soy bacon tastes just like real bacon," Ivy said.

"You've never had real bacon," Max shot back. "You can't make that claim."

"You've never had real bacon?" Kelly asked, surprised.

"Mom and Dad are vegetarians," Ivy explained. "I've never had meat."

"How come you eat meat if your family doesn't?" Kelly asked, turning to Max.

"Because I hung around with carnivores when I was a kid," Max replied, not missing a beat. "You know how some kids sneak other kids cookies in elementary school because some parents think sugar is evil? Well, my friends snuck me bologna sandwiches. They saved me from a life of broccoli and asparagus burgers."

"Huh," Kelly mused. "I never had anyone sneak me cookies. I didn't know people did that."

Ivy's heart rolled and when she risked a glance at her mother she saw Luna was feeling the same rush of empathy.

"You can have as many cookies as you want here," Luna said. "We never had meat in the house, but we always had Oreos."

"Thank you," Kelly murmured, studying her feet as her cheeks colored. She'd obviously revealed more than she wanted. That's when it hit Ivy: Her family's interference was a good thing. They were helping Kelly open up before she had time to think how to respond in a way that would help her remain hidden.

"Eat," Ivy instructed, tapping the edge of the girl's food container. "Eat as much as you want. I'll have Max go to the grocery store and get you some food that doesn't taste like broccoli and asparagus hamburgers, which I never made for him, by the way."

Kelly smiled thankfully. "Okay."

"**MAX** IS GOOD FOR HER," Ivy said, watching from the front porch as her brother showed Kelly where the resident raccoon was hiding behind the garbage cans along the side of the house.

"She doesn't seem scared of him," Luna mused, reclining on one of Ivy's front chairs.

"She's still leery around Dad, though," Ivy said. "Did you notice that?"

"And that's why I stayed sitting in the chair," Michael said. "I think … I think whoever hurt her was older."

"Like her father?" Ivy asked, tension building her in shoulders.

"Maybe," Michael said. "She seems comfortable with your mother and Max, and she's obviously already attached to you."

"I wouldn't go that far," Ivy said.

"I would," Michael said. "You might not have noticed, but she looked to you a couple of times for reassurance. Don't worry, Ivy. You gave it without even realizing what you were doing. It's instinctual with you."

"Your father is right," Luna said. "You were very good with her."

"Why do I sense a but coming on?" Ivy asked, her shoulders stiffening.

"Don't get your panties in a bunch," Luna warned.

"That's not what I'm doing ... and I hate that saying."

"Then don't make me use it," Luna said, unruffled. "Before you work yourself up, your father and I are not asking you to abandon this girl or stay away from her. If you think that's what we're doing, then hop off that crazy train right now."

"What are you suggesting?"

"She's not a pet," Luna said.

"I never said she was." Ivy was horrified. *Was that what they thought of her?*

"Ivy, one of the things I love most about you is your capacity to love," Michael said, his face somber. "You love with your whole heart and soul. That's why when you found Nicodemus in the Dumpster, there was no way you could ever let him go.

"Kelly isn't an abandoned kitten, though," he continued. "She's a teenager who has been through ... something. We don't know what yet, but if those bruises on her arms are any indication, it was something truly terrible."

"I know," Ivy said, furrowing her brow. "Why do you think I insisted that she stay here?"

"Because you want to help her," Luna said. "Your greatest gift – other than your insistence on being who you are without any reservations or compromises – is that big heart you have, Ivy."

"I don't understand what you're saying," Ivy said.

"We're saying that you can't get too attached to her," Michael said. "No one is asking you not to care. No one is asking you to throw her out, or turn away from her and let the professionals do their job."

"You can't fix everything, though," Luna said. "This girl needs help that you might not be able to give her."

"What do you want me to do?" Ivy asked, her voice cracking.

"Be you," Michael said. "Don't be afraid to ask for help, though. I'm here. Your mother is here. Max is here."

"Jack is here, too," Luna said.

"Oh, I'm so sick of hearing about Jack," Ivy grumbled.

"You're sick of hearing about him because you know we're right," Luna said. "That's also one of your … gifts. You're stubborn."

"Like a mule," Michael added.

"Well, thank you so much for that," Ivy deadpanned.

"Just be careful with your heart, Ivy," Luna said. "Life is full of obstacles. The ones Kelly is going to be facing over the next few days are going to be significant. You can't give her all of you because there will be nothing left to sustain yourself."

"I'm going to do what I have to do," Ivy said.

"I guess we can't ask more of you than that, can we?" Luna said, gripping Ivy's hand tightly. "Just keep your eyes open and your mind clear. If you're not careful, and you're not paying attention, something very important could slip by you."

"We'll be here to make sure that doesn't happen," Michael said. "We're here to help."

Her parents' words were sobering, and as Ivy watched Max and Kelly cavort with the raccoon she couldn't help but wonder if they were right.

Was she in over her head?

FIVE

"Are you sure you want to do this?" Ivy asked outside of the greenhouse door the next morning. "You can stay back at the house if you want. If you're scared to stay there alone, I can find someone to cover for me and stay there with you."

After a good night's sleep, Kelly looked better. The dark circles under her eyes were present, but fading. She was still too thin, but Ivy pumped her full of eggs and potatoes for breakfast in an effort to combat that. She was also still skittish, and when Ivy suggested she could work in the greenhouse all afternoon – away from prying eyes – she jumped at the chance.

"I'm sure," Kelly said, following Ivy into the greenhouse. "I want to do … something."

"Okay," Ivy said. "I'm always looking for someone who is willing to work for food." She winked at Kelly to let her know it was a joke.

After Max and her parents left the previous evening, Ivy tried to get Kelly to open up, but the girl was reluctant. Finally, Ivy let her be and tucked her in on the couch before retiring for the night. She was relieved to find Kelly still there in the morning. She didn't think the girl had anywhere to run, but when terror takes over, she knew there was no telling what a frightened soul would do.

"How did you get into plants?" Kelly asked, watching as Ivy gathered a handful of tools from the bench and directed her toward a stack of pots across the way.

"I don't know," Ivy said. "When I was a kid, I always knew that I liked the outdoors. I spent a lot of time in the woods with Max. We'd play games and run around. I liked to pick flowers, and I'd always bring them to my mother and she'd make a big deal about the gift. She acted like I brought her a gold necklace or something.

"My father always loved plants and he had a huge garden behind the cottage when I was younger," she continued. "We always had fresh everything ... tomatoes, green beans, carrots, onions. You name it, we had it."

"You don't have a garden like that now, though," Kelly pointed out.

"Once I decided to open the nursery, I realized I didn't have time to do both so I gave up the garden," Ivy said. "Dad has one at his house now, although it's not as big."

"It's kind of cool how you can walk to work," Kelly said. "Your house is great. It's hidden by the trees and yet it's not too far away from town."

"It is great," Ivy agreed.

"So, what do you want me to do?" Kelly asked, eyeing the pots and dirt nervously. "I should probably tell you I've never done anything like this before."

"It's lucky for you that I'm a good teacher then," Ivy said, patting the ground next to her. "Sit down. I promise it will be easier than you think."

JACK STRODE through the nursery aisles quietly, his dark eyes busy as he searched for Ivy. Despite her promise the day before she'd failed to call him once morning hit. Sure, the nursery was barely open, but he was itching to see if she'd discovered anything.

"Can I help you?"

Jack jolted at the sound of Michael's voice. "I'm looking for an irritating brunette with pink streaks in her hair and an annoying way of driving me insane."

Michael smirked. "I'm not sure I know anyone who fits that bill."

"Really? I believe she shares half of your genes."

"You make me laugh, boy," Michael said, clapping Jack on the shoulder. "You don't let Ivy bully you. Sure, she sweet-talks you to get her way, but she doesn't outright bully you. It's a nice change of pace."

Jack scowled. "She doesn't sweet-talk me."

"She did it yesterday afternoon," Michael countered. "You were adamant you were taking Kelly away and Ivy was equally adamant you weren't. Who won?"

"I … ." Jack broke off, frustrated. "Wait. Kelly? Ivy found out her name?"

"I think that's all she found out," Michael cautioned.

"Why didn't she call me?"

"You'll have to ask her that," Michael said. "I know she was planning on it. She probably just wants to get Kelly settled before she calls in the cavalry."

"She promised to call," Jack grumbled, running his hand through his hair.

"She's in the greenhouse," Michael said, biting the inside of his cheek to keep from laughing. There was something about Jack's hangdog expression that tickled his funny bone.

"Thanks," Jack said, starting to move in the direction of the greenhouse.

"Be careful when you approach," Michael said. "Kelly was fine with Max last night, but she's still skittish around men. I know you're a … cute little kitten … when my daughter is around, but you should still make sure you don't startle them."

"Cute little kitten?" Jack was incredulous.

"I guess you're more like a domesticated mountain lion," Michael clarified. "You're all growl and claws, but you also like to purr when you see something you like."

"Your whole family is just … unbelievable," Jack said, turning on his heel and moving away from Michael without a backward glance. "Un-freaking-believable!"

Jack managed to calm himself by the time he reached the greenhouse and since the door was already propped open, he didn't have to weigh the merits of knocking. He poked his head inside, resting it against the doorframe as he listened to Ivy instruct Kelly on the finer points of potting hydrangeas.

The two women were sitting cross-legged on the floor and Ivy was patient and even-tempered as she showed Kelly what to do. When the girl made a mistake, Ivy corrected her with soft tones and an absence of recrimination. When the girl did something right, Ivy applauded her and built up her self-esteem. It was a side of Ivy Jack hadn't seen before. She was usually aggressive and bossy – and oh-so sexy and cute. Today was no exception.

"Are you going to stand there and spy on us or help?" Ivy asked, not turning around even as she addressed Jack.

Jack sighed. "How did you know I was here?"

"I sensed you."

"How did you really know I was here?" Jack asked.

"I just told you."

Jack tamped down his irritation and sidled into the room, approaching the two girls slowly so he wouldn't scare Kelly. "I told you before that I believe you're magic," he said. "I'm not sure I believe you're clairvoyant, though."

"That's your problem," Ivy said.

Jack crossed his arms over his chest and waited.

"I also might have seen your reflection in the window," Ivy conceded, pointing toward the broad window to her right.

"That sounds about right," Jack said, shooting Kelly a small smile when he saw her eyes widen at their interaction. "Don't worry, Kelly. This is how we always get along. We're not fighting."

"We're not fighting," Ivy agreed. "Jack just likes it when I'm mean to him."

"That's not true," Jack said. "I happen to like nice women. I simply haven't met one since I arrived in Shadow Lake."

Ivy made a face. "I am perfectly nice to you."

"Whatever you say, honey," Jack said. "I don't suppose I could borrow you for a second, could I? Outside, please."

"I suppose," Ivy said, standing and dusting her pink ankle-length skirt off. "Keep potting, Kelly. I'll be back in a minute."

"Is everything okay?" Kelly asked uncertainly. "I'm not in trouble, am I?"

"You're definitely not in trouble," Jack said. "Ivy is another story."

"You're not going to … hurt her … are you?" Kelly's face was so anguished it caused Jack's heart to stutter.

"I would never hurt her," Jack said carefully. "I … never."

"Kelly, don't get upset," Ivy said. "Jack's telling the truth. He's a good guy. We just like to … argue. It's how we get along. He's a very good man. He would never hurt me or anyone else."

"Okay," Kelly said, her voice small and pitiful.

"Keep potting," Ivy instructed. "I promise I won't be gone long."

Once it was just the two of them outside, Jack's face shifted from worried to angry. "She's a mess."

"She was fine until … ."

"Until what?" Jack prodded.

"She didn't like us arguing," Ivy said. "She was honestly in a great mood until we started messing around with one another."

"Honey, just so you know, that's not how I mess around," Jack said.

Ivy's cheeks colored. "Are you flirting again?"

"I haven't decided yet," Jack said. "I … you frustrate me to no end."

"Right back at you."

"Great," Jack said, lifting his eyebrows. "Why didn't you call me this morning?"

"Excuse me?"

"You promised to call," Jack reminded her.

"I'm sorry," Ivy said, instantly contrite. "I was just getting her settled. She's not keen on being left alone. As soon as I distracted her with the hydrangeas I had every intention of calling you."

"And yet I had to come find you," Jack said. "See, this is exactly why I've declared my life to be 'woman free.'"

Ivy stilled. She knew he didn't mean for the words to be so personal, but that's exactly how she took them. "Don't worry. You won't have to worry about *this* woman infringing on your perfect little life."

Jack pressed his eyes shut, realizing what he'd said when it was too late to take it back. "Ivy . . . ."

"Don't worry about it," Ivy said, waving off whatever he was going to say. "You've been nothing but upfront with me. I don't want a relationship either."

Jack knew she meant that in theory, but both of them were having trouble staying away from each other. They were fighting their mutual attraction and that's why their conversations often devolved into sniping fits. "I didn't mean to hurt your feelings."

"Do I look like my feelings are hurt?" Ivy's voice was unnaturally high.

That's exactly how she looked and the realization was like a hot poker through Jack's heart. "Honey, I didn't mean that how it came out."

"Don't call me that," Ivy said.

"I . . . ." Jack pressed the heel of his hand against his forehead. This was a conversation he didn't want to have. This was exactly why he'd pledged to remain relationship free in Shadow Lake. He was no good to anyone, and despite her personality, he truly believed Ivy deserved the best this life had to offer. He just wasn't it. "I'm sorry. I … don't know what to say."

"I don't expect you to say anything, Jack," Ivy said, keeping her voice even and her eyes focused on a spot over his left shoulder. "I don't expect anything from you. We've been over this."

They had been over it … a few times. Then Jack couldn't stay away from her and opened the door again. He'd told her he merely wanted to hang out. He'd made it clear he didn't want a relationship. So why did he feel like such a loser? And why did he want to do nothing more than pull her in for a hug and tell her he'd made a mistake?

"Ivy, I'm a mess," Jack said honestly. "I'm more of a mess than that girl in there. As you can see, I take normal conversations and turn them into huge firestorms because I don't know what else to do. I'm ... sorry."

"I don't need you to be sorry," Ivy said, finally lifting her blue eyes to his. Jack saw hurt there even though she was trying to hide it. "I'm too busy for you. I'm also dumbfounded that you would even think I find you attractive."

She was giving him an out, but Jack's ego – and heart – couldn't take it. "Oh, please," he scoffed. "You're desperate to see me without my shirt on again. Admit it."

Since the first time he'd stripped his shirt off for her in her kitchen had been due to a nasty bout of Poison Ivy that sounded like a great idea to the feisty woman as she studied him. "I can make that happen," she warned. "I still remember where the Poison Ivy is."

Jack made a face. "That's not what I meant."

"I know exactly what you meant," Ivy said. "You're wrong, though. I don't want to see you with your shirt off. Frankly, I was horrified by your lack of muscle tone. It totally grossed me out."

Jack worked out six days a week and he was a walking wall of muscle with an eight-pack. He knew that wasn't true. Still, he was used to women falling all over him. Ivy was going out of her way to push him away, although he didn't blame her. "I've really let myself go," he agreed. "I'll get back in the gym first thing tomorrow."

"Good," Ivy said. "Was there something else that you wanted?"

Jack arched an eyebrow. "Believe it or not, I didn't come here to verbally spar with you. I need to know what you found out about your houseguest."

"Of course," Ivy said, feeling stupid for not remembering his true reason for coming to find her. "Her name is Kelly Sisto. She hasn't told me anything else. I don't know where she's from. I don't know what happened to her. She's slowly starting to trust me, but it's going to take time."

"You're going to keep her another night, aren't you?"

"Yes."

Jack ran his tongue over his teeth, debating how wise it would be to argue with Ivy. Finally, he decided he was going to let it go ... for now. "If she tells you anything, will you call me?"

"Yes."

"Will you make a point of doing it as soon as possible?"

"Yes."

"Okay," Jack said, cracking his neck and glancing around the nursery. "Just to be on the safe side, do me a favor and keep her away from the general populace until we know more."

"She's scared of the general populace."

"I know," Jack said. "Just ... be careful. Until we know who hurt her, we can't be sure that someone isn't looking for her."

"Oh," Ivy said, realization dawning. "You're worried someone is going to find her here, aren't you?"

"That's exactly what I'm worried about," Jack said. "If someone comes for Kelly you're going to make yourself a target. I don't want anything bad to happen to you, Ivy."

"I know," Ivy said. "Just because you don't want to date me, that doesn't mean you want me dead. I get it."

She was still hurt. Jack could practically feel it wafting off of her. "I ...."

"I don't want to go over this again," Ivy said, cutting him off. "I know where you stand. I'm not feeling sorry for myself and pining over you. You're good looking, but you're not irresistible."

Ivy pushed past Jack and moved back toward the greenhouse.

"I didn't say I was," Jack protested.

"Just ... get over yourself," Ivy said.

"You get over yourself," Jack grumbled under his breath, willing his heart to stop flopping around like a fish out of water. He had no idea what she did to him, but she always managed to leave him unsettled. It was starting to get frustrating.

SIX

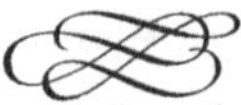

"Women are crazy."

Brian Nixon glanced up from his computer screen and focused on his partner as Jack stalked into the detectives' office at the Shadow Lake Police Department. "How is Ivy?"

Jack stilled. "Who said I was talking about Ivy?"

Brian snorted. "Son, I don't pretend to know you very well," he said. "I do know that Ivy Morgan has driven quite a few men to drink, though, and none of them has spent nearly as much time with her as you have."

"I'm not spending time with her."

"You played basketball with her," Brian said.

"That was one time."

"You've been sighted out at her nursery twice in the last week – this was before she found a traumatized teenager in the greenhouse – and I happen to know you're nowhere near ready to think about landscaping at the dump you live in," Brian said.

"I was just looking for ideas," Jack argued. "Wait ... how do you even know I was out there?"

"This town is full of gossips," Brian said, smiling at his younger partner. "My wife is in the loop. I'm pretty sure I already told you this."

"Nothing is going on."

"Oh, son, you're so cute," Brian said. "I know you believe that. I even know you want it to be true. You can't argue with chemistry, though, and you and Ivy are like a science experiment gone awry."

"Whatever," Jack said, throwing himself in his desk chair dramatically. "She's a pain in my rear end."

"She's got a way about her," Brian agreed. "Did she get anywhere with the girl last night?"

"Yes," Jack said. "We have a name to go on. Kelly Sisto. She didn't tell Ivy anything else, but it's somewhere to start."

"Well, let's see what we can come up with," Brian said, starting to type. "Are you going to sit there and daydream about Ivy, or are you going to help?"

"I'm not daydreaming about Ivy!"

"Keep telling yourself that."

"WHAT DO YOU THINK?" Jack asked from the passenger seat of Brian's cruiser as they studied the small ranch house from their spot on the street.

"It looks like a normal house," Brian said thoughtfully. "There are toys on the front lawn. The grass is long, but not so long they're risking getting a notice from the township."

After searching through state records, Brian and Jack found a sixteen-year-old girl with the same name who matched Kelly's description. She was living with a foster family – Derek and Emily Gideon – in a neighboring town, and from all outward appearances, the foster family didn't appear to be abusive.

Brian spent an hour on the phone with Kelly's caseworker, an overworked woman who said she dropped in on the Gideon household once a month. Brian worked overtime not to be accusatory, but he was well aware that state agency caseworkers had more files to follow-up on than hours in a day. Still, the woman insisted she saw Kelly on a regular basis.

"How do you want to do this?" Jack asked.

"Very carefully," Brian said. "We do not want to accuse these people if they're not guilty, and yet we need to be firm enough to scare them. We don't have any evidence, and it looks like there are more kids in this house. We have to be pleasant and act like we're merely trying to find answers, not trying to blame someone."

"I get it," Jack said. "Are you worried I'm going to fly off the handle?"

"I'm worried that an abused girl is going to set us both off," Brian said. "I'm saying it for my benefit, as well as yours."

"Let's do this," Jack said, pushing open his door and climbing out of the car. "The faster we get some answers, the faster … ."

"Ivy will be alone in her house again?" Brian suggested.

Jack scowled. "The faster we can help Kelly."

The woman who answered the door looked tired. She was dressed in simple jeans and a T-shirt, and her dark hair was pulled into a loose ponytail. She was holding a crying toddler in one hand, and another shy child was hiding behind her legs.

Brian pasted a bright smile on his face as he greeted the woman, flashing his badge to let her know it was an official visit. "Are you Emily Gideon?"

"Yes."

"Is your husband home?"

"He's in his office. Can I ask what this is about?" Emily asked, shuffling nervously.

"It's about Kelly Sisto," Brian said.

"She's at the library."

Jack and Brian exchanged a look.

"No, ma'am, she's not," Brian said. "Can you please get your husband? We have a few questions for you."

"But … we haven't done anything," Emily said.

"Ma'am, get your husband."

. . .

DEREK GIDEON WAS a short man with a big waistline. His ample stomach hung over his waistband, and his round face was red as he greeted Brian and Jack with a welcoming – and yet forced – smile.

"How can I help you?"

"We need to ask you some questions about Kelly Sisto," Brian said, shaking his head when Emily offered him a glass of iced tea. "We understand that she's your ward."

"She's been living here for the past fifteen months," Derek said. "Has she done something?"

"No," Brian said. "We're trying to find out what happened to her."

"I'm not sure what you mean," Emily said, clasping her hands on her lap. "Nothing has happened to her."

"When was the last time you saw Kelly?" Jack asked.

"This morning," Emily said. "She got up early and said she was going to the library to read. She doesn't like to spend a lot of time with the younger kids."

"Ma'am, we know that's not true," Jack said. "Kelly didn't spend the night in this house."

"I … ." Emily broke off, biting her lower lip and shooting a look in her husband's direction.

"What's going on?" Derek asked.

"Kelly was found in Shadow Lake yesterday," Brian said. "She was hiding in a greenhouse at a local business. Her arms were bruised, and she was traumatized to the point where she screamed when anyone tried to approach her."

"I … that's not possible," Derek said. "She has a curfew. She has to be in this house by nine every night."

"And you're saying you saw her last night?"

"Of course," Derek said. "We're diligent foster parents. We take care of the kids the state places with us. I don't know what you think … ."

"I'll tell you exactly what I think," Jack interrupted. "I think you take kids from the state to get the paycheck. I don't think you've seen Kelly in days, maybe weeks even. I think you're trying to cover your asses, but it's not going to work because we've had Kelly for the past twenty-four hours. Stop lying."

"Don't you dare accuse me of anything," Derek snapped.

"We're not accusing you of anything," Brian said, shooting Jack a dark look before focusing back on the Gideons. "I raised a few teenagers. I know how troublesome they can be. We need to put a timeline together, though. Something happened to Kelly, and we need to know what."

"Why don't you just ask her?"

"She's not keen on talking right now," Brian said.

"What happened to her?" Emily asked.

"We're not sure yet," Brian replied. "She's … adjusting … right now. When she's ready to talk, she'll talk."

"She should be with us," Derek said. "We're her guardians."

"She's … good where she's at," Brian said.

"She's safe," Jack added.

"Are you insinuating she wouldn't be safe here?" Derek asked. "We're good foster parents. We take this job very seriously."

"Obviously," Jack replied dryly. "A good foster parent always lies to law enforcement about a child in their care."

"Hey, you have no idea what we're dealing with here," Derek said. "We've got four mouths to feed under this roof, and that's not counting us. Kelly is a teenager. She doesn't need constant supervision."

"No one was suggesting she did," Brian said. "The fact remains that Kelly has been gone for at least twenty-four hours. You either knew and didn't report it or you didn't know. I'm not sure which prospect is worse, quite frankly."

"Kelly doesn't always stay here," Emily said.

"Shut up, Emily," Derek snapped.

"No," Emily said, shaking her head. "She's a teenager. She kind of … comes and goes as she pleases."

"I thought she had a curfew," Jack said.

"She does," Derek said.

"Okay, I've had just about enough of this," Brian said. "When was the last time you saw Kelly? If you say this morning … or last night … I'm going to have a caseworker out here every day for the next month, even if I have to pay them out of my own pocket."

Jack arched an eyebrow, surprised and impressed.

"We saw her four days ago," Emily said, resigned. "She stopped in to get some fresh clothes and do some laundry."

"How often does she stay here?"

"A couple nights a week."

"Where does she stay the other nights?" Jack asked, rampant dislike for the Gideons rolling through his stomach.

"She has a few friends," Emily said. "She usually sleeps on their couches or … I don't know … maybe she has a boyfriend."

"Are you saying you have no idea where she spends her nights?"

"She's here two or three nights a week," Emily said. "She comes in after we've gone to bed most of the time. Then she eats breakfast with us and takes off again."

"As long as she keeps her grades up and is here for social worker visits, we kind of let her do her own thing," Derek said. "She's an easy kid. She doesn't get in trouble, and she doesn't talk back."

Jack made a face, disgusted. "Well, don't worry about seeing her again," he said, getting to his feet. "She'll be relocated. I can guarantee that."

"Wait a second … ."

"No," Jack snapped. "She's a teenage girl, not an adult. You guys paid so little attention to her you didn't even know she was missing. We're done here."

"No, we're not," Brian said. "I'll be notifying the state about the situation in this house as soon as I get back to the office. If I were you, I'd be expecting a visit. Something tells me your status as foster parents is going to be studied rather closely."

"I want to see Kelly," Emily said. "I'm sure, if you give me a chance to talk to her, I can work this all out. We are not bad people."

"I have no idea if that's true or not," Brian said. "I do know that you're negligent people. Don't leave the area. I have a feeling we're going to be back for another chat once Kelly is ready to open up. Even if you don't see us, though, you're going to be seeing some people who look a lot like us."

"You can't do this," Derek said. "You're messing with our livelihood."

"Sir, don't ever tell me what I can and can't do," Brian said.

"I THOUGHT you said to remain calm," Jack said once they were back at the cruiser.

"Is that guy still standing?"

Jack nodded.

"Then I remained calm," Brian said, clearing his throat to ward off his disgust. "Can you believe those people didn't even know she was missing?"

"Sadly, I've seen situations like this before down in the city," Jack said, referring to his former life as a Detroit police detective. "You would be horrified to see some of the foster home situations I've seen."

"I understand that," Brian said. "I don't condone it, though. That girl could've been killed and they never would've been the wiser as long as they had the checks to cash."

"Well, she's out of there now," Jack said. "Do you think they're the ones who hurt her?"

"I don't know," Brian said. "They seem more lazy than anything else. They don't seem particularly smart either. I just ... don't know."

"We need Kelly to start talking," Jack said.

"We can't force her," Brian said. "I don't know everything, but I do know that. Kelly needs to feel safe before she confides in anyone. Ivy is our best chance, no matter how much that bugs you."

"It doesn't bug me," Jack countered. "I know Ivy is a good person. It's just ... she drives me crazy."

"That's hormones, son," Brian said, winking. "The only way Ivy Morgan is going to stop driving you crazy is if you give in and embrace the hormones."

"That's not going to happen."

"It's going to happen," Brian said. "You're not ready yet, but you'll get there. I have faith."

"I really dislike you sometimes," Jack grumbled, climbing into the cruiser.

"You'll live."

SEVEN

Where am I?

Ivy was dreaming again. Instead of the woods surrounding her house, though, she was on a dark street. She didn't recognize her surroundings, the tall buildings jutting into the sky marring the skyline and serving as a gentle reminder that she was in a city – which she rarely went to if she could help it.

She had nothing against cities, she reminded herself. They were just dirty, loud, and annoying. She disliked the very idea of them. She liked to run free, her long hair trailing behind her as she raced through the forest. Cities smothered, they didn't enhance.

So why was she dreaming about one now?

"I'm not making excuses, Mom. I really do have to work on Sunday."

Ivy recognized the voice, turning her head expectantly as Jack strolled down the sidewalk on the other side of the street. He had a cell phone pressed to his ear, and he seemed oblivious to his surroundings. Ivy knew she had attitude where cities were concerned, but this didn't look like a safe neighborhood. She opened her mouth to call after Jack, hoping his presence would cut back the shadows that appeared to be encroaching on her, but something caught her attention out of the corner of her eye.

Someone was following Jack.

Ivy couldn't make out the dark silhouette's features. It was clearly a man, broad shoulders tapering down to a narrow waist and sturdy thighs. He was tall. Not quite as tall as Jack, but tall all the same. He moved furtively, purposely keeping himself in the shadowed alcoves offered by the various fire escapes littering the brick façade of the nearby buildings.

Without realizing what she was doing – or why – Ivy followed. Her bare feet padded along the cement silently, and even though she knew it was a dream, she couldn't help but hope she wouldn't step in anything disgusting during her trek.

"Mom, I'm not being difficult," Jack said, continuing his conversation. "I honestly have to work. I'm not just saying it because I don't want to have Sunday dinner with you. That's ridiculous."

Jack stopped in the middle of the sidewalk, and even though she was behind him, Ivy could read the frustration as it settled on his shoulders. "Mom, I promise, as soon as my workload lightens up, I'll carve out a special day for you. It's just ... this is a big case."

He was silent for a few moments as he listened to the woman on the other end of the line.

"I'm not trying to be a bad son, Mom," Jack said. "I'm trying to be a good cop. No ... no ... you just talk to hear yourself talk sometimes, don't you?"

Ivy couldn't stop herself from smiling. Despite the exasperated look on Jack's face, the love for his mother was evident. He looked lighter in this dream, like the troubles of his past weren't weighing down his future. That's when Ivy realized where she was. This was a dream, but it was one that stemmed from a real incident.

The dark figure trailing Jack increased his pace while Jack argued about the merits of familial love. Suddenly, Ivy knew exactly what memory Jack was stuck in, although she had no idea how she'd been drawn into it. That's what was happening, though. She was a visitor in his dream.

Almost as if she was in someone else's body, Ivy watched in horror as the figure drew something out his pocket. It was a gun. Someone was about to shoot Jack. She'd seen the scars on his chest. She knew whoever it was hit his target. Ivy opened her mouth, desperate to change history even though she knew it wasn't possible.

"Jack!"

JACK BOLTED to a sitting position in his bed, his heart hammering as a cold sweat clung to his bare chest. He'd had the dream so many times he'd lost count, and yet this one had been different.

He'd been walking down the street talking to his mother. They were arguing about the fact that he'd missed three family dinners in a row. The dream was always the same. The conversation was always the same. Everything happened just like it did on that fateful night.

Until tonight. Tonight was different. This time, just when he was about to find out who his true enemy was, someone called his name. In the split-second before consciousness claimed him, Jack caught a glimpse of the woman trying to save him – and he would've recognize that dark hair with the pink streaks anywhere.

Ivy.

Jack rubbed the back of his neck, pushing the remnants of the dream out of his head, and glanced out his bedroom window. Morning was here, although barely. He knew it was fruitless to try and return to slumber. Once he was up, he was up. He couldn't go back under with the dream so fresh in his mind.

Jack tossed the covers off of his body, stretching as he climbed to his feet. He caught a glimpse of his reflection in the mirror over his dresser, his eyes automatically dropping to the twin scars on his chest. They were located a few inches from his heart, and they served as constant reminders that trust and loyalty were earned, not given away freely.

Ivy gave him a bottle of cream two weeks before, claiming it would help the scars fade. At the time, he'd told her he didn't want the scars to fade – but that wasn't the truth. He wanted them gone. If he could shake the mental ones, that would be even better. It was those scars keeping him from Ivy now. He wasn't the same man who was shot in that dream, though, and the man looking back at him from the mirror wasn't worthy of a woman like Ivy.

Jack pressed his eyes shut briefly, picturing her beautiful face and pouty lips. There was just something about her. He couldn't explain it. He couldn't identify why he was drawn to her. He wasn't so obtuse that he didn't recognize the attraction every time it zinged him. He also wasn't brave enough to push the fear out of his mind and give in so he could claim what he really wanted.

No, Jack Harker knew he wanted Ivy Morgan. He didn't need his subconscious to tell him that he was looking at her as a form of salvation. He could feel it every time they shared oxygen. That didn't mean he was going to give in, though.

She deserved a real man. She deserved someone who wouldn't be forever scarred by the sins of the past. She deserved someone who could love her completely.

Jack didn't think he was any of those things.

"**GOOD** MORNING, HONEY."

Ivy made a face when she saw Jack outside her front door. After she'd rudely walked in his dream the previous evening, she felt odd being in his presence. She'd invaded his personal space. There was no doubt about that. Instead of apologizing and owning up to her indiscretion, though, she opted to ignore it.

"What are you doing here so early?"

Jack held up a brown diner bag, shaking it enticingly. "I brought breakfast."

"Why?"

"Because that's what people eat in the morning," Jack replied, unruffled by her grouchy behavior.

"But why?"

"Because I need to talk to Kelly, and I thought breakfast would make it easier," Jack admitted.

Ivy bit her lip, conflicted. She knew Jack had a job to do. She also knew Kelly wasn't ready to be pushed. "I don't know."

"If you're worried about me seeing you with bedhead, don't," he said. "I've already seen you in the morning."

"I don't have bedhead."

"If that's your story ... ."

Ivy self-consciously ran a hand through her hair, internally sighing when she realized it was standing on end in some places. "You get off on this, don't you?" She pushed open the door, resigned.

Jack couldn't help but smile when he saw her fuzzy pajama pants and tank top. She was adorable in the morning. She looked muddled, and her mind wasn't firing on all cylinders without her morning caffeine fix, and he just wanted to ... touch her. "I think you're cute in the morning."

"That's just what every woman wants to hear," Ivy said, turning on her heel and stalking toward the kitchen. "Hey, you look ... cute."

"It's better than looking like a crazy person," Jack said, walking into the living room and closing the door behind him. He scanned the couch, remnants of Kelly's night scattered about in the form of a pillow and blanket. "Where is Kelly?"

"She's in the shower," Ivy said. "I let her take the first one because the water doesn't hold out for two and I don't want her to suffer."

"That must've made mornings hard when you were a teenager," Jack said, following her into the kitchen and resting the bag of food on the table. "Did you and Max battle it out every morning?"

"No. Max was stronger than me, so he usually rubbed my face in his armpit and then held me down until I gave in."

"And your parents let him get away with that?"

"My parents never got involved in our fights," Ivy said. "Once we hit a certain age, they said we had to battle it out on our own."

"Did you ever win?"

"Sure," Ivy said. "Sometimes I tied his door shut with a piece of rope from the outside."

"That sounds fun," Jack said, smirking. "Wait ... this house only has two bedrooms. Where did Max sleep?"

"There's a bedroom in the basement," Ivy replied, yawning as she measured coffee grounds. "Max lived down there."

"I didn't know this place had a basement," Jack said. "That's good. It's kind of small otherwise."

"It's perfect for one person," Ivy corrected. "When four of us were living here, it was rough, though."

"What do you have in the basement now?"

"Nothing."

"Nothing?"

"If you must know the truth, I'm kind of scared of the basement," Ivy said, snapping the drawer into place and pressing the button to start the coffee machine. "I had nightmares about being locked down there as a kid, so I rarely went down there unless I was desperate for a good shower."

"You're scared of your own basement? I didn't think you were scared of anything," Jack teased, settling at the kitchen table.

"Everyone is scared of something, Jack," Ivy said. "Everyone."

Jack met her serious gaze for a moment, confused. While she definitely wasn't a morning person, she usually wasn't so melancholy either. "What's wrong, honey?"

Ivy shook her head, dislodging the serious thoughts. "Nothing is wrong. It just takes me a little bit to wake up in the morning. What's up with you? Why are you here with the crows?"

Jack glanced over his shoulder to see if anyone was listening. When he found the hallway empty, he turned his attention back to Ivy. "We found Kelly's foster parents yesterday."

"Foster parents?"

Jack nodded.

"Where are her real parents?"

"They died in a car accident when she was eight," Jack said. "She's been in the system ever since."

"That's horrible."

"It is," Jack agreed, fighting the urge to reach across the table and take her restless hand into his.

"Did they ... do something to her?"

"I don't know," Jack said. "They didn't even appear to know she was missing." He told Ivy about his visit with the Gideons the previous afternoon, keeping the story short but hitting all the important beats. When he was done, he waited for her response.

"What a bunch of jackholes."

He wasn't disappointed. "They're definitely ... jackholes," Jack agreed. "Wait ... is that supposed to be a slur where you use my name?"

"Not everything is about you," Ivy said, tapping her finger against his chin and causing his face to warm. "I've always called people that."

Jack wasn't sure he believed her, but he let it go. "Has she mentioned anything about being in foster care?"

"No."

"I need to talk to her about this," Jack said, choosing his words carefully. "I know you don't want me to, but I can't put it off."

"She's so scared, Jack," Ivy said. "She doesn't trust you yet. She barely trusts me."

"I know," Jack replied. "That's why I'm going to be working out here today with both of you."

"Excuse me?"

"I'm working out here," Jack said firmly. "I'm going to go out to that greenhouse and ... pot whatever you want me to pot ... and just generally get to know her before I have to start asking her some tough questions."

"You're going to pot plants in my greenhouse all day?"

"Did I stutter?"

"Do you really think this is a good idea?" Ivy asked. "If you and I spend an entire day together we're either going to kill each other or ... ." She broke off, her cheeks coloring as she refused to finish the statement.

Jack didn't finish it for her either. He knew exactly what she was going to say. They were going to either kill each other or kiss each other. He knew it, too. "I don't know what else to do. I really want to help her."

Ivy sighed, tugging her hand through her snarled hair dejectedly. "Will you promise to do what I say and let me be the boss?"

Jack felt a little thrill in his stomach at the suggestion. "If that's what you're in to."

Ivy scowled. "You know very well that's not what I meant."

Jack reached for the bag of food and started doling the eggs, potatoes, toast and sausage out. "If that's your story."

"I hate men sometimes," Ivy grumbled.

EIGHT

"This makes absolutely no sense," Jack said, staring down at the pot Ivy was shoving in his direction and shaking his head.

"What confuses you?" Ivy asked, irritated.

"That plant is already in a pot."

"I noticed."

"If it's already in a pot, how come I have to put it in another pot?" Jack asked.

"Because I said so."

Jack scowled. "Why really?"

Ivy sighed. "Plants have delicate root systems," she said. "If you let the root system of a particular plant get too big in a small pot it becomes warped and hard to deal with. If you put the plant in a bigger pot, the roots can spread."

"Okay, let's say I buy that in theory," Jack challenged. "If that's the case, then why don't you just put these things in big pots to begin with?"

"Because that's a waste of space," Ivy replied. "Besides that, if you put a tiny plant into too big of an ecosystem, it can flounder and die."

"You're just making that up."

Ivy narrowed her eyes and extended her index finger menacingly in his direction. "You said you were going to do what I said."

"No, I said that you clearly got off on being bossy and I was going to let you dominate me today," Jack countered. "Those are two totally different things."

"You're impossible," Ivy snapped, tossing a dirt-covered gardening glove in his direction.

Jack caught it in midair. "You throw like a girl."

"You shoot hoops like a girl," Ivy shot back.

"You cheated," Jack said. "You had home court advantage and you know it."

Kelly giggled, caught up in the interplay.

Jack and Ivy shifted their attention to her, surprised.

"This is not funny," Ivy said.

"It's funny," Kelly replied. "You two are like a bickering old couple. I can see you in fifty years sitting on the front porch of the cottage and arguing about who is right and who is wrong."

"I'm always right," they said in unison.

"See," Kelly said. "It's so … cute."

"I am not cute," Jack said. "I am manly and strong and should be treated thusly – even by a woman who wants to dominate and degrade me."

"Who is degrading you?" Ivy asked, frustrated.

"You are," Jack said. "You're talking down to me because I don't know how to pot a plant."

"You always talk down to me."

"I do not."

"You do, too," Ivy said. "You treat me like I need a babysitter. Admit it."

"You're so full of it your eyes are turning brown," Jack said. "I've treated you with nothing but respect since the day we met."

"Oh, really?"

"Yes, really."

"What about the night you insisted on sleeping on my couch even though I didn't want you to?" Ivy asked.

"I slept on your couch because a crazy person left you poisonous flowers," Jack argued. "You were in danger."

"I was not in danger."

"Oh, really? Were you, or were you not, stalked in the woods by a crazy person?"

"You were stalked by a crazy person?" Kelly's eyes were as big as saucers.

"Technically yes," Ivy said. "However, I was not stalked that night. I wasn't stalked until the next night."

"Did you ever consider you weren't stalked that night because I was sleeping on your couch?" Jack asked.

"I … ." Ivy's mouth hung open as she mulled the question over. "Oh, crap. I hate it when you're right."

Jack wrinkled his nose. "Did you just admit I was right?"

"No."

"You did, too," Jack said. "Where is my phone? I want you to repeat that last statement for me while I record it. Every time you argue with me about who knows best, from now on, I'm going to play that back for you."

"You are crazy," Ivy said, pushing herself to her feet and dusting off the seat of her cargo pants. "I am not repeating that. In fact, I never said it at all. Kelly is my witness."

"Kelly is my witness," Jack said, reaching for Ivy's leg as she moved around him. "Where are you going? I'm not done winning this argument yet."

"You haven't won this argument. I … oomph." In her haste to get away from Jack's insistent hands, Ivy took too long of a stride and her foot landed on a metal dowel, causing her to slide along the floor and topple forward.

Jack instinctively reached up and caught her, using his impressive muscle mass as a buffer to protect Ivy from a hard impact on the greenhouse floor. Ivy gasped, rolling over in Jack's arms so she could face him. Their faces were inches apart.

"I'm sorry," Jack said, fighting to keep his heartbeat in check. "I … I shouldn't have grabbed you like that. You could've been hurt."

"You caught me," Ivy said, surprised. "I … you actually caught me."

"It's not like I cured cancer," Jack said, embarrassed and yet pleased at the way she was looking at him. "I … you were right there. I just reached out for you."

"Well, thank you," Ivy said, wrinkling her nose. "Jack?"

"Hmm." Her eyes – and the feeling of warmth she was bringing to his chest as he cradled her close – mesmerized him.

"I think you should probably let me up."

"Okay." He didn't move to release her.

"We have an audience," Ivy reminded him.

Reality intruded on Jack's happy thoughts. "I'm sorry," he said, loosening his grip and helping Ivy to a standing position. "I don't know why I did that."

"Me either," Ivy said, arching an eyebrow.

"I know why," Kelly offered.

Ivy and Jack shifted their attention to the teenager.

"You're hot for each other," Kelly said.

"We are not," Ivy said.

"That's absolutely the furthest thing from my mind," Jack scoffed.

"Whatever," Kelly said, rolling her eyes. "Max told me you two are playing a game. I didn't know what he meant when he said it, but now I do."

"We're not playing a game," Jack said.

"I'm going to beat the crap out of Max," Ivy said.

"I'm going to help," Jack added.

"Yeah, I'm going to side with Max on this one," Kelly said. "He's clearly right about you two, whether you want to admit it or not. In fact, I'll bet Max is right about everything."

Ivy made a face. "Max is not right about anything," she said. "Whatever he tells you, do the exact opposite."

"He told me you would say that," Kelly said. "When is he going to stop by again, by the way?"

"Never," Ivy replied. "He's banned from my house."

"Do you really mean that? Would you really just stop talking to your brother?"

Ivy stilled. "No," she said, realizing Kelly's upbringing was vastly different from her own. "No matter how angry I am with Max, he's still my brother. I'll love him until the day I die … and beyond. We like to fight. That's what brothers and sisters do."

Kelly glanced at Jack for confirmation.

"I'm going to agree with Ivy on this one," Jack said. "My older sister and I fought like cats and dogs. That doesn't mean we don't love each other."

"I didn't know you had a sister," Ivy said.

"You never asked."

"I … I guess that's fair," Ivy conceded. "Where does she live?"

"She lives down in Macomb Township," Jack said. "It's a suburb of Detroit, but it's far enough north that it doesn't look like the city."

"Where did you live when you were down there?"

"Detroit."

"Did you have to live in the city because you were a police officer there?" Ivy asked.

"Yes."

"Did you like it?"

"You're asking a lot of questions all of a sudden," Jack said. "You weren't interested in my past before."

"I was interested," Ivy said, her voice soft. "I just didn't want to … push you."

Jack's face softened. "You're not pushing me," he said. "I … what do you want to know?" He had no idea why he was opening the door to this conversation, and yet he didn't want to close it.

"Did you like the city?"

"I liked being able to go to a grocery store … or a movie … or even a gas station in the middle of the night if I wanted to," Jack said. "You can't do that in Shadow Lake."

"No," Ivy agreed.

"I didn't like all of the … concrete, though," he said. "I didn't like all the people. I didn't like all the smog. I didn't like all the crime."

He didn't like being stalked in the dark and shot twice, Ivy added silently. "Do you like it up here?"

"I like parts of it very much," Jack said pointedly, his gaze fixed on Ivy's face. "I like the open spaces, trees, fields, and rivers. I like the quiet. I like a lot of the people."

"Like Ivy?" Kelly teased.

Jack cocked an eyebrow as he regarded the teenager. She'd grown steadily more accustomed to his presence over the course of the afternoon. She wasn't exactly comfortable with him yet, but she was getting there. "I like Ivy sometimes," he said. "I want to strangle her sometimes, too."

"Not really, though?"

"Not really," Jack said. "I know you don't know me, Kelly, but I would never hurt anyone. I wouldn't hurt you, and I definitely wouldn't hurt Ivy."

"Even if she ... called you a name?"

"She's called me plenty of names," Jack said. "In fact, she denies it, but I think she's turned my name into an insult of sorts."

"I told you that I've been calling people jackholes since I was a kid," Ivy argued.

"I'm not sure I believe you."

"And that's why you're a jackhole," Ivy said.

Jack smirked, despite himself. "See."

"I think you're nice," Kelly said after a moment. "I think you're nice to Ivy, too, even if you guys like to pretend you hate each other."

"We don't hate each other," Ivy said. "We're just ... combative."

"We're both bossy," Jack explained. "Ivy is used to getting her way, and so am I. When you put two people who think that way together, they fight."

"I think it's more than that," Kelly said. "I think you two want to kiss each other."

Ivy pressed her lips together, conflicted. "I'd rather kiss a toad."

"I'll find one for you so we can test that theory," Jack said, narrowing his eyes.

"My foster parents never kiss each other," Kelly said, lost in thought. "They never look like they want to either. I guess I just thought that's how all adults acted around each other. You two are proving me wrong."

There was the opening he was looking for. Jack cleared his throat. "Speaking of your foster parents, I had a talk with them yesterday."

Kelly froze, her face a mask of fear and doubt. "W-what did they say?"

"Well, first off, they told me you were at the library," Jack said, refusing to lie. "When I pointed out that was impossible, they opened up about a few things. They weren't happy about it, though."

"Are they going to kick me out?"

"I don't think you need to worry about that right now," Jack said. "They have bigger fish to fry. Besides, I thought you were happy here with Ivy for the time being?"

"I am," Kelly said hurriedly. "It's just … they don't like it when kids make waves. They want kids to be good … and quiet."

"I kind of figured that out myself," Jack said. It was now or never. "Kelly, I need to ask you a question."

"You want to know if they hurt me, don't you?"

"Yes."

"They never touched me," Kelly said. "They're not bad people. I know you probably look at them and see … jackholes … but they're not horrible people. I've been in a lot worse foster homes than that one."

The admission caused Jack's heart to flip. "Well, we're going to make sure you have a stable home when this is all said and done."

"Derek and Emily really aren't bad people," Kelly repeated. "They're just … limited."

"Kelly, they're not foster parents because they care about kids," Jack said. "They're foster parents because the state pays them to be. They weren't watching out for you."

"No one is a foster parent because they like kids," Kelly said. "Well, I guess there probably are some good foster parents out there. I've never met them, though."

Jack exchanged a brief look with Ivy. She looked just as upset as he felt. "Are you sure your foster parents didn't hurt you?"

"I'm sure," Kelly said. "I'm not going to pretend they were great role models. I'm not going to make up a lie and say they got me a Christmas gift every year. They didn't hurt me, though. It's not in their nature. You don't have to worry about that."

That was a relief … sort of. "Who did … ?"

Ivy cut off the rest of the question with a shake of her head. A quick look at Kelly's downtrodden face told Jack she was right. Now was not the time to press Kelly further. She'd opened up a little. Now he had to reward her.

"So, who wants ice cream?"

"You've barely done anything," Ivy said.

"I've put up with you for two hours," Jack said, chucking her under the chin. "I think that definitely means I deserve ice cream. Who wants me to make a Dairy Queen run?"

NINE

"How does pizza sound for dinner?" Jack asked, walking out of Ivy's bathroom after washing his hands and face and moving toward the living room. "I don't know about anyone else, but I'm starving."

"You're inviting yourself to dinner?" Ivy asked from the couch.

"No, I'm offering to pay for dinner and let you eat some," Jack countered.

"I love pizza," Kelly said, her gaze bouncing between Ivy and Jack worriedly. It was almost as if she was waiting for them to explode. Truth be told, Jack was waiting for it, too.

"Fine," Ivy said, too tired to put up a fight. A full day of potting – and verbally sparring with Jack – had left her weary. "I want my own pizza if you two are going to get meat, though."

"I can live with that," Jack said. "We'll get a large with all the fixings – including meat – for Kelly and me, and you can have some vegetable monstrosity all to yourself."

"Great," Ivy said. "I love pizza when it doubles as an inedible monstrosity."

"You would," Jack said. "You order."

"Why me?"

"Because I'm not familiar with the pizza joints in town yet," he said. "I figure you know which places are good and which ones are bad."

"That shows what you know," Ivy grumbled. "There's only one pizza place in town."

"Of course there is," Jack said, rolling his eyes as he settled in the armchair and watching Ivy get to her feet and shuffle into the kitchen.

"Kelly, is there anything you don't like on your pizza?" Ivy asked.

"I'll eat anything."

"That's not an answer," Ivy prodded.

"I … um … don't like anchovies."

"No one does," Jack said. "Do you like pepperoni?"

Kelly nodded.

"Ham? Onions? Mushrooms?"

Kelly nodded at each question.

"That's what we want on ours," Jack said. "Extra cheese, too."

"How can you possibly eat that and look like you do?" Ivy asked, nonplussed.

"I work out."

"You wouldn't have to work out as much if you ate better," Ivy said.

"No one asked for your diet critique," Jack said. He leaned over and reached for the remote control. "Do you like baseball, Kelly?"

"Not really."

"You just haven't watched it with the right person," Jack said. "I'll explain the game to you and you'll be a fan in no time."

"I understand the game," Kelly said. "I still think it's … kind of slow."

Ivy snorted. "She means it's boring."

"No one asked you, honey," Jack said, winking at her. "Now, be a dear and order our dinner. I wasn't joking when I said I was starving."

"Be a dear?"

"That's what I said, honey," Jack said. "Be a dear."

"I'm going to have them add spit in your pizza," Ivy threatened, but she reached for the telephone. Kelly was having far too good of a time to end the evening now.

"I don't want spit on my pizza," Kelly said.

Ivy made a face.

"What? You told me to tell you what I didn't want on my pizza," Kelly said.

It was the first joke she'd made, and Ivy was obliged to laugh. Jack joined in, and when the three of them were done laughing, Ivy placed the call. Putting up with Jack's mouth – and his incredible body and handsome face – was well worth getting Kelly to smile.

"SHE SEEMS TO BE ADJUSTING," Jack said, reclining in one of the plastic lawn chairs on Ivy's front porch and watching Kelly as she sat on the wooden swing beneath Ivy's massive maple tree.

"She does," Ivy agreed. "She's still scared, though."

"She's opening up," Jack said. "I … was wrong about her staying with you. You've done wonders for her. I don't think anyone else could've done what you have in such a short amount of time."

"Did you just admit you were wrong?" Ivy asked, snickering. "I might have misheard. I just want to make sure I heard what I thought I heard."

"You are such a pain in the ass."

Ivy waited.

"Did you hear that?" Jack asked.

"I did. I'm still waiting for you to say I was right again."

Jack sighed. "You were right, Ivy."

"Can I go inside and get my phone and record that?"

"Only if you're do the same for me," Jack challenged.

"I'm comfortable right here."

"That's what I thought," Jack said, shifting his eyes from Kelly's back to the stars. "It's beautiful here. You forget how many stars there are in the sky when you live in the city."

"Does the smog blur them out?"

"Not in Detroit," Jack said, chuckling. "Don't get me wrong, the air quality sucks – especially when it's hot and everyone is running their air conditioners – but it's not like Los Angeles."

"What is it like?"

"Ah, we're back to the questions," Jack said.

"I'm sorry. You're entitled to your privacy. I shouldn't invade it."

"Honey, you've been one of the most respectful people I've ever met when it comes to my privacy," Jack said. "You've gone out of your way to ... ignore ... the scars on my chest. You haven't asked the big questions everyone else is dying to ask. Instead, you've just sat back and let me do my own thing."

"That's because I'm an amazing person."

"You're egoless, too," Jack teased, glancing over at her. His heart almost lodged in his throat when he saw her features under the muted glow of the moon. She was breathtaking.

Ivy shifted so she was facing him, her face unreadable. "What happens to Kelly now?"

"Now you keep doing what you're doing," Jack said. "Make her feel safe. When she's ready, she'll tell us what happened."

"What do you think happened?"

"I honestly have no idea," Jack said, his gaze never wandering from the fathomless depths of her blue eyes. "I ... oh, honey, you're so beautiful it hurts to look at you sometimes."

Ivy stilled, surprised at the statement. "What?"

"I can't help it," Jack said. "You drive me crazy. There are times I literally want to gag you. You're still the most beautiful woman I've ever seen in real life."

"You didn't need to add the 'in real life' caveat at the end," Ivy said, her eyes twinkling.

"I just ... ." Jack leaned forward, his lips pressing to Ivy's softly as he lost himself in a moment he couldn't give back.

Ivy was surprised by the kiss, but she returned it. There was something about the moon that always mesmerized her. Jack's face was hypnotic under the worst of circumstances – and this was anything but. It was a magical night, and they both gave in to the magical moment.

After a few seconds, Jack pulled away with a rueful expression on his face. "I shouldn't have done that."

"I know."

"I ... why did you let me?"

"Because I can't stop myself either," Ivy admitted. "It's like I lose all sense of reason when you're around."

"Are you admitting that because of the moon?"

"I have no idea why I'm admitting it," Ivy said. "I ... can't seem to lie to you."

"You told me you thought I was hideous with my shirt off," Jack teased.

"Yes, but even you knew that wasn't the truth," Ivy said.

Jack sighed and leaned his head back so he could stare at the stars. "You're ruining my plan. You know that, right?"

"What plan?"

"The one where I was supposed to move up here, take a job at a boring police department, spend my days and nights working on a craphole house, and never look at a woman."

"You haven't exactly been good for my life plan either," Ivy said.

"What was your life plan?"

"Building my nursery up to the best in the county, reading as many books as I can get my hands on, and never looking at a man again."

"That sounds like a lonely existence, honey," Jack said. "I think you deserve more."

"See, you're looking at me and thinking that I deserve a happily ever after," Ivy said. "The thing is, you're not looking at the potential men in this equation and realizing that I can never make any of them happy."

Jack leaned forward, flustered. "What does that mean?"

"I'm odd, Jack," Ivy said. "I know it, and you know it. People in town call me a witch, and for all intents and purposes, I am one. I might not cast spells. I might not ride around on a broom. I might not curse my enemies. I do believe in magic, though."

"Honey, every time I look at you I believe in magic," Jack said. "I don't think you see yourself like others see you, though. You could make someone very happy if you'd open yourself up to the possibility."

Ivy shifted uncomfortably. "Just not you, right?"

"I … I don't know what you want me to say," Jack said, hating himself for the paralyzing fear coursing through him. "I like you. I do. You make me laugh, and you're beautiful. I am not in a place where I can offer you what you deserve, though."

"I'm not saying I want you," Ivy said. "Don't think that's what I'm saying, because if your ego gets any bigger it's not going to fit on this porch. For the sake of argument, though, what don't you have to give me?"

"All of me."

"Why?"

"Because I left part of me on the pavement in Detroit as I was bleeding out."

It was one of the most honest things Jack had ever said to her, and it crushed a little of Ivy's spirit. "Do you dream about it every night, or was last night a special occasion?"

Jack stilled. "What?"

Ivy realized what she'd said, but it was too late. "Nothing. I … um … I should probably check on Kelly." She moved to get to her feet, but Jack's hand shot out and wrapped around her wrist.

"How did you know I dreamed about it last night?"

"Um … I don't know. It was just a guess." Ivy licked her lips, her throat dry as blood rushed to her cheeks. How was she going to get out of this? She'd let her big mouth get away from her. Again.

"Were you in my dream last night?" Jack queried, stunned he was even asking the question.

Ivy rubbed the heel of her free hand against her forehead. She was caught. "Yes."

"How?"

"I don't know," Ivy replied truthfully. "I don't know how I got there. I didn't even know where I was until I saw you on the sidewalk."

"What did you see?" Jack was having trouble wrapping his mind around the conversation.

"I saw you on your cell phone," Ivy said, fighting back tears. "You were arguing with your mom about missing family dinner."

"How could you possibly know that?"

"I was there. I don't know why. I think ... I think you might have called to me in your sleep."

"That's not possible," Jack said, releasing her wrist and cracking his neck. "That's ... just not possible."

"How do you explain it then?" Ivy asked, irritation starting to bubble up. Was he calling her a liar? "I've been having dreams about you for the past week. Most of the time they're stupid. We watch a sunset together ... or take a walk in the woods ... or visit my fairy ring."

Jack's head snapped up, surprise draining his face. "What?"

"I thought that's the type of dream I was having last night," Ivy said. "I didn't realize I was in your dream until ... well ... I saw the man behind you. He had a gun."

"Holy crap," Jack said, getting to his feet swiftly. "Are you telling me all those dreams I had – holding hands by the fairy ring, watching the sun set in your back yard – are you telling me that all really happened? Were we sharing those dreams?"

Now Ivy was on her feet. "You had those dreams, too?"

"Are you telling me you didn't know?"

"I thought they were my dreams," Ivy said. "I didn't know we were sharing them."

Jack wanted to believe her. She looked so vulnerable he was fighting the urge to pull her into his arms and soothe her with a hug. After all, he'd just found out all the hugs and kisses he'd dreamed were shared by both of them. He couldn't help but feel betrayed, though.

"You're in my head," he said, taking a step back. "How? Is this some witch thing you do?"

"I don't know," Ivy said, frustrated. "I've never done it before. I honestly didn't know we were in each other's dreams together. I thought ... I thought they were just mine."

"You knew you were in my dream last night," Jack pointed out.

"Not until it was almost over."

"Why didn't you say something?"

"I didn't want to scare you," Ivy said, chewing on her lower lip.

"Scare me? Ivy, you're not scaring me. I … this is a violation."

"I'm sorry." Ivy knew it was a lame apology, but she didn't know what else to do.

"I have to go," Jack said, moving toward the steps that led down from her front porch.

"I … shouldn't we talk about this?"

"I need to think," Jack said, refusing to turn around. "I'll … be in touch."

With those words, Jack Harker raced to his truck and climbed in. He cast one more look at Ivy, his heart rolling at the crestfallen look on her face, and then he fired up his engine and pulled out of her driveway.

He had no idea what to do with this information. Every time he called Ivy "magic," he'd meant it in a flirty way. Now it turned out she really was magic, and he had no idea what to do with the revelation.

TEN

"How come Jack left without saying goodbye?" Kelly asked, helping Ivy fix up the couch before bed a few hours later.

"He had someplace to be."

"He looked upset," Kelly said.

"He was just … distracted." There was no way Ivy could explain Jack's mood without telling Kelly why he was so thrown. She didn't want to scare the girl, especially when she had no way of knowing how she was walking in Jack's dreams.

"Did I do something? Is he mad at me? That's it, isn't it? He doesn't like me." Kelly's lower lip quivered.

"That's not it," Ivy said, faltering. She had to constantly remind herself that Kelly was fragile. "He's mad at me. It has nothing to do with you."

"I don't believe you," Kelly said. "He likes you. You can tell that every time he looks at you."

"Kelly, I swear, he's angry at me," Ivy said. "I did something to him."

"What?"

Ivy licked her lips, unsure how to answer. "I … invaded his privacy in a way that upset him," she said. "I didn't mean to. It was an accident."

"Why doesn't he understand that it's an accident?"

"It's hard for him to wrap his mind around," Ivy said. "He's a good man. He just needs some time to think."

"But ... how did you invade his privacy?"

"It's not easy to explain," Ivy said. "Jack is a private person. He's had a ... rough time of it. Like you. He doesn't want to talk about it."

"Like me," Kelly said.

"Yes," Ivy said. "I said something I shouldn't have said. He's not mad at you. I can promise you that. He's mad at me."

"Will he forgive you?"

"I don't know," Ivy said. The truth was, if their positions were reversed, she wasn't sure she could forgive him. "He'll be okay. He'll still want to talk to you. Don't worry about that. Jack isn't the type of man who just abandons someone."

"He abandoned you," Kelly pointed out.

"No, he didn't. He got angry and needed some time to himself," Ivy said. "No matter what you think about Jack, never doubt that he's a good man. He's one of the best men I've ever met, in fact. If I needed Jack, he would drop everything and come running."

"Even though he's upset?"

"Even though," Ivy said, nodding. "Are you ready for bed? Do you need anything before you go to sleep?"

"No," Kelly said, hopping onto the couch and watching as Ivy pulled the blanket over her. Nicodemus jumped up onto the couch, turned three times, and then planted himself on Kelly's feet. It was as if he was watching over her. Even though Ivy missed him in her bed, she knew the cat understood that Kelly needed him more right now.

"I'll see you in the morning," Ivy said. "How about I make pancakes?"

"Sure," Kelly said. "That sounds nice."

Ivy started moving toward the hallway. "I'll be right down here in my bedroom if you need me. My door will be open."

"Thank you for letting me stay here."

"You're more than welcome. Trust me. I like having the company."

. . .

IVY WAS in Jack's dream again. She knew it the second she "woke up" on the gritty city streets. Most dreams have a filmy quality, but since this dream was actually a memory, Jack saw it with acute clarity. That meant Ivy did, too.

"Oh, no," Ivy said, glancing around worriedly. "This is not going to prove I'm trustworthy. I don't want to be here. I want to wake up."

"You can't wake up. That would be too easy for both of us." Jack's voice was hollow as he moved up beside her, his eyes lifeless. "You're here again. Why?"

"I don't know," Ivy said. "I don't want to be here. I'm so sorry."

"What happens now?"

"It's your dream, Jack. I'm just a visitor."

"You think I somehow brought you here, don't you?"

Jack looked tired, and despite her worry that he would pull away, Ivy reached out and touched his cheek. He felt real. If she didn't know she was in a dream, she would think he was standing beside her.

Jack pressed his eyes shut and leaned into her touch for a moment. "Why can I feel you?"

"I don't know."

"Something is happening here, Ivy. I can't … I don't … please, tell me what is going on. Tell me how to get you out of my head."

"I don't know how to stop this," Ivy said, her voice plaintive. "You're calling to me. That's all I know."

"Why are you coming?"

"Because I don't know how to stop myself from coming to you," Ivy said. "I'm so sorry."

"I know," Jack said. "I just … I can't deal with this. It's too much. This is my nightmare. You shouldn't be here. You shouldn't … see."

"I'll stay here. I … won't follow you. When you wake up, I should be catapulted out of the dream."

"I can't leave you here," Jack said. "It's not safe."

Ivy chuckled darkly. "Jack, this is your dream. I know it feels real, but it's not. I can't die in your dream."

"I … I guess I never thought of that."

"You can't die either," Ivy whispered. "You've already survived this."

"Have I?"

"Jack … ." Ivy's heart was breaking. "I don't know what to do for you. I feel like I'm intruding, and yet I can't walk away because it's your dream. You're keeping me here for a reason. Why?"

"I obviously want you to see," Jack said. "This is what this is all about, right?"

"Maybe," Ivy conceded. "Maybe you want someone to understand what you've gone through. Maybe you want to share your pain."

"I don't want you to see," Jack said. "I … you don't deserve it. This is my nightmare."

"I'm stronger than I look, Jack. I can stay here and wait for you to wake up, or I can go with you. It's up to you."

Jack instinctively reached out and clasped Ivy's hand. "I won't let anything happen to you."

Ivy wished she could give him the same reassurance. "I have faith in you. You should know that just because something bad happened to you, that doesn't mean it should define you."

"Are you going to get philosophical on me in my dream?"

"Are you going to pick a fight in your dream?" Ivy shot back.

"You're a piece of work," Jack said, gripping her hand and leading her down the sidewalk.

"Where are we?"

"Detroit."

"Duh." Ivy made a face. "Where in Detroit?"

"Mack Avenue, close to Gratiot."

"Is this a bad area?"

"It depends on your definition of 'bad.' From your point of view, I'm guessing this whole city is a bad area."

"I try not to be judgmental," Ivy said.

Jack snorted. "Since when?"

"I don't think I like your attitude."

The sound of footsteps on the pavement cut the hot retort on Jack's lips short, and when Ivy stiffened, he gripped her hand tighter.

"It's okay, Ivy. I never hear him until he's already on me. If you hear something, it's not danger."

"I don't want to watch you being shot," Ivy said.

"I don't know how to save you from that. Can't you wake yourself up?"

"Can't you?"

"I try every night," Jack said. "It hasn't worked so far."

"Why do you keep coming back to this dream, Jack? Do you blame yourself for what happened?"

"I don't know," Jack said. "I think I blame myself for not seeing what was going to happen. Does that make sense?"

"I still don't know exactly what happened," Ivy reminded him. "I … know you were shot twice. I know someone close to you betrayed you. I know you almost died."

"How do you know all of that?" Jack asked. "Can you read my mind?"

"I'm not magic, Jack."

"You're magic. I knew it from the second I saw you," Jack said. "I just didn't know you were this … magical."

"I'm not magical," Ivy said.

"You believe in magic. You have your own fairy ring. Your aunt claims she can see auras. I'm starting to think you're more than you let on. I'm starting to think you're more than even you believe."

"You're dreaming, so I'm going to let that go," Ivy said. "You sound like a fortune cookie, though."

Jack shot her a small smile. "See, that right there proves you're magic. You can make me laugh right before someone comes to kill me."

"Jack … ." Ivy was lost. She didn't know what to do. "You can change this. It's your dream." She clutched at his hand desperately. "Think of someplace else. Think of the happiest place on Earth. You can make yourself go there right now. This doesn't have to happen again."

"It's too late, Ivy," Jack said, staring down at her soulfully. "He's already here."

Terror gripped Ivy's heart. Intellectually, she knew she was safe. The fear was real all the same. "Don't turn around."

"I have no choice," Jack said. "We have to have a conversation. I've had it hundreds of times now. It never changes. I always want answers to the same question. The funny thing is, I know he's not going to tell me what I want to hear."

"What do you want to hear?"

"I want to know why he's doing it. I want to know why he did … what he did."

"What did he do?" Ivy was curious, even though she'd promised never to press Jack on the subject.

"He betrayed his family. He betrayed the city. He betrayed … his badge. He betrayed me."

"You were shot by another police officer?"

"Jack!"

Ivy cringed when she heard the voice. She knew what was coming and she was desperate not to see it. Jack cupped the back of Ivy's head and brushed a quick kiss against her forehead. "You need to move over there now."

"I'm not leaving you." Ivy's voice was firm.

"You can't stop this, Ivy," Jack said. "You said it yourself. It's already happened."

"No," Ivy said, shaking her head vehemently. "We can stop this together. Stay with me. Don't engage him. If you try, we can go to another place."

"Stay here, honey," Jack said, his smile wan. "It won't take long."

"No," Ivy said. "I … oh … ."

"What's going on?" Jack asked, surprised to see her face draining of color.

"I'm waking up," Ivy said. "I … ."

"Good," Jack said. "This is my nightmare." He let go of her hand. "It will be okay. I know what to expect."

. . .

IVY BOLTED TO A SITTING POSITION, her heart pounding and her breath coming out in raspy gasps. "I have to get back to Jack," she said.

Kelly's hand was icy as it gripped her arm.

"What's wrong?" Ivy asked, shifting her gaze to Kelly as she tried to clear the muddled mess that was her mind. She longed to be back with Jack, and yet she knew he wasn't really where she left him. Kelly was here now, and if her face was any indication, she was terrified.

"There's someone at the front door," Kelly whispered, sobs choking her. "Someone's trying to get in."

"Are you sure?" Ivy asked, tossing the covers from her body.

"He's here," Kelly said.

"Who?"

"He's going to kill me. He told me he would." Kelly was openly sobbing now.

"No one is going to kill you," Ivy said, grabbing Kelly by the shoulders. "I promise you that." She grabbed her cell phone off the nightstand and punched in Brian Nixon's number without hesitation. She pressed the phone into Kelly's hand and directed her toward the closet. "Tell him what's going on. Tell him to come."

"What about you?"

"Don't worry about me," Ivy said. "I can take care of myself."

Ivy closed the closet door behind Kelly and then turned in the direction of her dark hallway. This was her home, and there was no way she was going to let anyone take Kelly from it.

No matter what.

ELEVEN

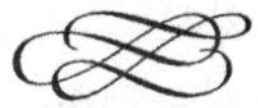

"You look like hell," Brian said, glancing up from his computer as Jack settled at his desk in the detectives' office the next morning. "Late night?"

"Something like that," Jack muttered.

"With Ivy?"

"I was not with Ivy last night," Jack said. Technically, that wasn't a lie. Sure, she'd walked in his dreams and almost bore witness to the worst moment of his life, but that all happened in his head. It didn't count.

"I know you weren't," Brian said, nonplussed.

"I see your spies are still on top of their game."

"Nope. I know you weren't with Ivy last night because I was with Ivy last night."

Jack stilled, surprised and confused. "What? Why?"

"Someone tried to break into her house," Brian said.

"What!"

"Kelly called from the closet in Ivy's bedroom," Brian said. "Ivy locked her in before she went to investigate the noise herself."

"I'm going to kill her," Jack seethed. "Wait ... is she okay?"

"You should probably have expressed those sentiments in the

opposite order," Brian said. "She's fine. I went out there. It looked like someone tried to jimmy the lock on her front door and the bedroom window, though."

"Sonovabitch," Jack swore. "Were they looking for Kelly?"

"That's the assumption I'm working on," Brian said. "I don't think Ivy has ticked off anyone in the past few days – other than you, that is – so that means it has to be because of Kelly."

"Who knows she's out there?"

"Besides you and me? Just her family."

"Someone else has to know," Jack pressed. "What about the state? When you reported the Gideons, who did you talk to?"

"I reported the situation to the state police."

"Did they ask where Kelly was?"

"They did. I told them she was in a safe foster care environment until we could get answers from her."

"And they were okay with that answer?"

"They didn't put up a fight," Brian said.

"That means someone either followed Kelly to Ivy's property or managed to find out some other way," Jack said.

"It does."

Jack turned and stalked toward the door.

"Where are you going?" Brian asked, already knowing the answer.

"You know where."

"Try not to kill her," Brian said. "I'd hate to have to arrest you."

"No promises."

JACK WORKED to keep his temper in check as he hopped out of his truck and moved up Ivy's driveway. Movement drew his attention to the side of her house, and when he strode to the area in question, he found Max busily studying the outside of Ivy's window.

"What are you doing?" Jack asked.

"Trying to figure out how to beef up the security here," Max said. "Any suggestions?"

"I have a few ideas," Jack said. "I need to talk to your sister first. Where is she?"

Max's face was unreadable as he looked Jack up and down. "You don't look well, man. Have you been sleeping?"

That was a thorny question, and one Jack had no intention of answering. "Where is Ivy?"

"She's on the back patio with Kelly," Max said. "Be forewarned, she's in a bad mood. I don't think she slept either."

"I don't doubt that," Jack said. "I'm going to send Kelly over here to help you, so don't be surprised when she shows up." Jack moved around Max and walked in the direction of Ivy's back yard.

"Are you and my sister going to scream at each other?"

"No."

"Do you want to scream at her?" Max asked.

"You have no idea," Jack said.

He found Kelly and Ivy drinking iced tea on the patio a few moments later, and Kelly was on her feet and heading in his direction before he had a chance to register her exuberance. She threw her arms around his neck. "Ivy told me you wouldn't just abandon us."

Jack patted Kelly's back awkwardly. "I wouldn't do that." His somber eyes landed on Ivy. She looked as uncomfortable as he felt. "I'll always come when you're in trouble, Kelly. Don't worry about that."

"That's what Ivy said."

"Ivy is smarter than she looks sometimes," Jack said, forcing a grin. "Can you go and help Max with the window? He's just on the side of the house over here."

"Do you want to talk to Ivy alone?" Kelly teased, obviously missing the fraught look on Jack's face.

"I do," Jack said.

"Are you going to make up?"

"We're not fighting."

"Ivy said you left without saying goodbye yesterday because she did something to upset you," Kelly said.

"I ... I wasn't upset," Jack said. "I was ... sick."

"Sick?"

"I had a stomachache from eating too much pizza."

"You're lying," Kelly said, not missing a beat. "I'm not going to invade your privacy and ask why, though. Ivy says you don't like that." She turned to Ivy. "Is it okay if I go and help Max?"

Ivy nodded. "Do me a favor and make sure he's not doing anything goofy."

"I can't do the impossible," Kelly said, excitedly moving around the side of the house.

Jack remained where he was until he saw Max greet Kelly and then he moved over to the patio with Ivy. "Are you okay?"

"I'm fine," Ivy said, exhaling wearily as she leaned back in her chair. "How are you?"

"I'm not here to talk about me," Jack said. "I'm here to talk about you. Did you see anyone?"

"No," Ivy said, shaking her head. "I was asleep … ." Her cheeks colored as she met Jack's even gaze. "Then I woke up to Kelly shaking me. She was terrified. I put her in the closet and handed her the phone so I could check on it for myself. I didn't see anyone when I opened the door."

"You opened the door?" Jack was already edgy for most of her story, but he practically exploded at this tidbit. "What were you thinking?"

Ivy shrank back, surprised. "I … ."

"I didn't mean to scare you," Jack said, holding up his hands. "I'm sorry I yelled that loudly. I just … why didn't you climb into the closet with Kelly? Why did you go looking for trouble?"

"I wasn't looking for trouble, you … butthead," Ivy said, making a face. "I didn't know if she imagined it. Besides that, I didn't have anything to protect us in that bedroom. If someone was trying to get in, I needed a knife from the kitchen."

"That's not what you were doing, and don't call me a butthead, by the way," Jack said. "You were going to sacrifice yourself to protect Kelly. Don't even bother denying it."

"You are a butthead," Ivy said, jumping to her feet. "I was trying to do what I thought was right."

"Stop calling me that!"

"Then stop acting like it!"

Jack crossed his arms over his chest, exhaling heavily through his nose. He sounded like a bull readying to charge, and the thought wasn't completely out of the realm of possibility. He just wasn't going to charge and gore her. No, he was going to charge at her, grab her by the shoulders, and kiss her senseless. *No, wait, where did that come from?*

"I didn't come here to fight with you," Jack said, choosing his words carefully.

"You always come here to fight with me," Ivy said, her voice softening. "I think you like it."

Jack was starting to think he liked it, too. "I ... about last night ... ."

"You don't have to say anything," Ivy said, waving him off. "I don't need an apology."

Jack made a face. "Who said I was going to apologize? You're the one who invaded my dreams."

"You're the one who keeps calling me into them."

"That's what you say. How do I know you're telling the truth?" Jack knew he was being purposely bratty, but he needed to put the crumbling wall to his heart back in place. She was making inroads at a disturbingly high rate of speed, and he was starting to panic.

Ivy reared back as if she'd been slapped, and Jack immediately regretted his words. "This is why I don't get involved with anyone," she said. "I'm weird. Weird things happen to me. It's all fun and games when men see something different about a woman. It's something else entirely when they have to deal with it."

"Don't even go there," Jack said. "That's not what I was saying."

"What were you saying?"

"Just that ... Ivy ... I ... ." Jack was at a complete loss. He had no idea how to deal with this situation. It was crippling him.

"I'm sorry you keep calling me into your dreams," Ivy said, her blue eyes nothing more than dangerous slits. "I don't know why you're doing it. You might want to look inside yourself for that answer. I'm not the one doing it."

"I'm not magical."

"Neither am I."

Jack couldn't put a name to what was going on, but knew that wasn't the truth. "I think you are."

"I think you're crazy," Ivy said. "I think you want someone to blame for every crappy thing that's happening, and I'm just a convenient target."

"That is not true!"

"Whatever," Ivy said, placing her hands on her hips. "I am truly sorry you feel I've … betrayed you. I know that's a hot-button issue for you. I am not doing it on purpose. I would never consciously betray you." Her eyes were glistening with tears, and even as she fought them, Jack's knees almost buckled. He couldn't bear to see her cry. "I'm sorry this is happening. I really am. I don't know how to fix it, though."

"Ivy, I'm sorry," Jack said. "I know this isn't your fault. I just … I don't know how to deal with this."

"That makes two of us."

Jack pressed his lips together and turned to the horizon, where the sun was high in the sky and yet shadows still shrouded his heart. "Why didn't you call me?" He hadn't meant for the question to come out like an accusation, but the look on Ivy's face told him that's exactly how she was taking it.

"Excuse me?"

"You were in trouble last night," Jack said. "You called Brian. Why didn't you call me?"

"I … ." Now Ivy was the one at a loss for words. "You stormed off. You were angry with me. I didn't know how you would feel about me calling. I just … reacted."

"You saw me after I left, though," Jack said. "I still don't know how, but you were in my dream. You told me you were waking up. I was relieved at the time. I don't understand why you didn't call me when you were in trouble."

"Maybe because I don't want you to feel you have to save me," Ivy said. "You've been very clear about how you feel. You don't … want me. I can't keep calling you because then you'll think I'm trying to force a situation that I'm not."

"I wouldn't think that."

"I don't believe you."

They were at a crossroads. This was Jack's chance to walk away. "When you're in trouble, you need to call me. I don't care whatever cockamamie girl-power idea you have swimming through that crazy head of yours. I can't bear it if something happens to you. When something bad happens, you damned well better call me from here on out."

"Don't tell me what to do," Ivy warned, irritably tapping her bare foot on the patio. "You're not the boss of me."

"Oh, stuff it," Jack said.

Ivy's face was murderous. "Excuse me?"

"You heard what I said."

"I don't have to stand here and take this," Ivy said.

"So, why are you?"

"Because … well … this is my property. If anyone should leave, it's you."

"I'm not leaving," Jack said. "In fact, I'm going to go help Max make sure this house is secure. How do you like them apples?"

"You're a butthead."

"I've heard." Jack couldn't help but enjoy watching the hot flush creeping up her neck. He knew it was more than anger fueling her. He wondered if she realized it, too.

"I don't need you to keep my house safe," Ivy said. "I don't want you here."

"I don't remember asking what you wanted," Jack said.

"I … you … we … you're a butthead!" Ivy had nothing else to do now but make a dramatic exit. Jack watched her storm into the house with a small smile. When he turned his head back to the side of Ivy's house, he found Max and Kelly staring at him.

"That sounds like it went well," Max said.

"Your sister is a lunatic."

"She is," Max agreed. "I'm starting to think you're one, too."

"I am perfectly sane."

"That's why you're smiling because you sent her over the edge," Max said.

"I'm doing no such thing," Jack said. "She needed a good talking to. She has to know going after a possible intruder in the middle of the night is not allowed."

"Hmm," Max said, his tongue in his cheek. "Is that why you were upset? I thought it had more to do with the fact that she called Brian instead of you."

"I ... how long were you listening?"

"You guys don't do anything quietly," Max said. "We heard most of it."

"How much is that?"

"Some of it we didn't understand," Max conceded. "I'm not sure what the dream stuff is, but it sounds like you two have quite a bit going on these days."

"Just let it go," Jack said. "Let's go have a look at all the windows and doors. I'm not leaving this house until I know it's safe."

"Yes, sir," Max said, clicking his heels together and mock saluting.

"It's cuter when your sister does it," Jack said, moving toward the side of the house. "Let's start over here and work our way around."

Kelly's hand shot out as Jack moved past her, timidly grabbing his forearm. Jack stilled, lifting his eyebrows as Kelly nervously regarded him.

"What's wrong, kid?" Jack asked, forcing himself to remain calm even though Ivy still had his stomach twisted in knots.

"When I woke her up last night she said something."

Jack waited.

"She said she had to get back to you," Kelly said. "She was frantic about it."

Jack's face softened. "Okay," he said. "I ... I'll deal with that. Don't worry about Ivy. She's just persnickety. She'll calm down in a little bit."

"She likes you," Kelly said.

"She's got a funny way of showing it."

"She's scared you're going to break her heart," Kelly said.

Jack cocked an eyebrow. "Did she tell you that?"

"No. Sometimes you can just tell things by looking at people, though. When she looks at you, she's scared. When you look at her, you're scared. Maybe you guys should stop fighting things separately because it makes you scared. If you fight them together, who knows, you might find some courage."

Jack was dumbfounded as he watched Kelly shuffle down the side of the house. When he lifted his face, he found Max staring at him.

"Out of the mouths of babes," Max said.

"Oh, don't you start," Jack said. "Come on. Let's make sure this house is secure. I have a feeling whoever came here last night isn't going to stop after one try."

TWELVE

"Fancy meeting you here."

Jack glanced up from the beer he was nursing at Denny's Bar several hours later, surprised to see Max sliding onto the stool next to him. This was his first time frequenting a drinking establishment since relocating to Shadow Lake, and he was expecting to wallow alone.

"Did you follow me?" Jack asked, arching an eyebrow.

"No," Max said. "I come here three nights a week. The female clientele misses me when I don't show up." Max winked at two blonde women sitting in a nearby booth. When they started giggling, Max shot Jack a knowing look. "See."

"Wow," Jack said, making a face. "It's like you're a dating guru or something."

"Don't make fun of my dating prowess," Max said. "I'm a legend around these parts." He focused on the owner behind the bar. "How's it going, Denny?"

"Well, I'm still alive," Denny said, the light from the top of the mirror at the back of the bar glancing off his bald head. "I consider that a good day."

"It sounds like it," Max said, grinning. "I'll have whatever is on tap."

The two men sat in silence until Denny delivered Max's drink and ambled farther down the bar to wait on several other customers. While Jack was happy with the silence, Max was not.

"Do you want to tell me what's going on with you and my sister?"

"Nothing is going on," Jack said, tracing his finger through a line of condensation on the bar top. "I wish people would stop assuming something is going on."

"You know why people assume that, right?"

"Because this town is the size of my shoes and they have nothing better to do?"

Max barked out a hoarse laugh. "Partially. They also assume it because no one can be in the general vicinity of you and Ivy and not feel the fireworks when you look at each other."

"Ugh." Jack made a disgusted sound in the back of his throat. "That is such crap. Don't get me wrong, I'm fond of your sister. She says what she thinks, and she means what she says. I don't have feelings for her, though."

"You keep telling yourself that," Max said. "Maybe you'll believe it in about fifty years or so."

"Whatever." Jack averted his eyes from Max's probing gaze.

"My sister is just as guilty as you are in this situation," Max said. "Don't think I'm taking her side and blaming this all on you."

"Your sister is a piece of work."

"She's definitely a piece of work," Max agreed. "She's also one of the best people I know."

Jack swallowed hard. "I don't know what you want me to say."

"I want you to tell me why you're so desperate to stay away from my sister," Max said. "I want you tell me what happened to you."

Jack stilled. "What do you mean? What did your sister tell you?"

Max held up his hands, warding off Jack's potential fury. "She didn't tell me anything," he said. "Well, that's not entirely true. When I was teasing her about having a crush on you, she said you'd been through something terrible and there was no way you could have feelings for her so I should let it go."

"She didn't tell you what happened to me?"

"No. Why do you think I'm asking you?"

"I have no idea," Jack admitted, hanging his head. "I can't … get her out of my head. Literally. She's in my head."

"She has an annoying habit of being able to do that," Max said.

"No, that's not what I mean," Jack said. He glanced around the bar to make sure no one was eavesdropping. Other than the girls in the booth, who were staring at the two men like they were hamburgers and they hadn't eaten in weeks, no one was paying attention to them, though. "Has your sister ever … I don't know … shown you that she has actual magical powers?"

Max practically spewed the beer he was sipping out of his mouth. "What?"

"Does she have … abilities … that she's not telling anyone about?"

"You're starting to freak me out, man," Max said. "What is going on?"

Jack didn't know what to do, so he told Max about his dreams – including Ivy's cameos. He didn't tell him about the shooting, and he blurred some of the details about his ordeal, but when he was finished, Max was flabbergasted.

"Are you putting me on?"

Jack shook his head.

"What does Ivy say?" Max asked, genuinely confused and surprised.

"She says that I'm calling her to me," Jack replied.

"Do you believe that?"

"I don't know what to believe," Jack said. "I know I can't be in a relationship right now. I'm no good to anyone, especially your sister. I don't know what to do, though. She drives me crazy. I can't stay away from her."

"That's because you're attracted to her," Max said. "Don't worry. She's attracted to you, too. I've never seen her like this with another guy. It's like you get her so worked up she has no choice but to explode. Unfortunately for you, she keeps exploding all over you."

"That's a nice visual," Jack muttered.

"I know you don't want to tell me what happened to you, and I'm okay with that," Max said. "Frankly, it's none of my business. It sounds to me like you want to share it with Ivy, though. Have you considered that?"

"No."

"Well, as long as you're looking at it from a healthy perspective, man." Max patted Jack's arm, nonplussed, and twirled around so his back was leaning against the bar and he was on full display for his fan club in the booth. "You know, when I first heard you were moving to town, I thought you were going to be competition."

Jack lifted an eyebrow. "How?"

"Well, as you can see, I'm quite popular with the female population in Shadow Lake," Max said. "According to Ava Moffett, who got a glimpse of you when you were interviewing, you were hot and ready and she was going to nab you.

"Now, I don't care who nabs Ava … or Maisie, for that matter … but I was worried you were smart enough to see beyond them and start encroaching on my turf," he continued. "I figured I was going to have to beat you up if that happened."

"If I remember correctly, you did try to beat me up when we first met," Jack said.

"That's because I didn't know who you were and I thought you were going to murder my sister," Max said. "Let's not make the story more than it is, shall we?"

Jack smirked. "Fine. I'm not interested in being your competition, though. You know that, right? I don't want to date anyone. I came to Shadow Lake to be by myself."

"I know," Max said. "The problem is, you ran smack dab into my sister and all of your good intentions and quiet dreams flew out the window. I know you don't want to have feelings for her. I also know you do have feelings for her. Your head and your heart are at war, man. Sooner or later, one of them has to win or you're going to drive yourself insane."

"I don't want to hurt your sister," Jack said. "Not for anything."

"Of course you don't," Max said, chuckling heartily. "You're a good guy. I hate to admit it, but you are. I never thought anyone would be good enough for my sister, but I'm starting to rethink that."

"Well, I'm not," Jack said. "I know I'm not good enough for your sister. She deserves more than what I can give her."

"My sister deserves the world," Max agreed. "She's not willing to take it for herself, though. Someone is going to have to give it to her. And, for someone to give it to her, she's going to have to let that someone get close to her. The only one who has even made it through her front door is you. That has to mean something."

"It means we're both idiots," Jack said, swigging from his beer.

Max studied him for a moment, a myriad of ideas floating through his head. Finally, he settled on a course of action. "Do you really want to get over my sister?"

"There's nothing to get over."

Max made a face. "Don't push me, man. I'm trying to help you."

"Fine. What do you suggest?"

"Come on," Max said, climbing off the barstool and grabbing Jack's arm. "There are two distractions right over there, and they're primed for the plucking."

"I just told you I didn't want a relationship," Jack argued.

"Who said anything about a relationship? Those are just two women to flirt with. You can be my wingman."

"I don't know."

"You're coming," Max said. "If anyone can take your mind off my sister, it's one of those two. Trust me. In an hour, you won't even be able to remember Ivy's name."

Max knew that wasn't true. He knew the two women at the table. They were vapid, catty, and overly sexual. He knew twenty minutes with them was going to be enough to send Jack out of the bar as if his hair was on fire. He was just hoping that inclination would also make him see that his heart was already taken, and maybe it would be unwise to throw that away without giving it a chance.

. . .

"SO, WHAT IS THIS MOVIE?" Kelly asked, sitting on the couch next to Ivy and reaching into the bowl of popcorn.

"It's called *Dirty Dancing*."

"Is it old?"

"From your perspective, yes," Ivy said. "From my perspective this is a movie my mother always watched when I was a kid and I fell in love with it. I have no idea why."

"Okay," Kelly said dubiously. "What's the deal with the music, though? There's no beat."

Ivy smirked. "This was what music was like before hip hop came along."

"Is this the kind of music they had when the dinosaurs were around?" Kelly teased.

"Pretty close," Ivy said.

"Hey, that's the grandmother from *Gilmore Girls*."

"It is," Ivy said.

"Who is the hot guy?"

"His name is Patrick Swayze," Ivy said. "And if you think he's hot now, wait until you see him dance."

"Has he been in anything recently?"

"No," Ivy said, shaking her head. "He died a few years ago. If you like this, though, I can scrounge up a few other things he was in. Wait until you see *Ghost* … and *Point Break* … ooh, and *Red Dawn*."

"Do you watch a lot of old movies?"

"My mother loved movies," Ivy said. "I don't consider them old. She always let me watch them with her. I would curl up on the couch with her, just like you're doing now, and we would watch them."

"That sounds nice."

"It was," Ivy said, her eyes drifting to Kelly's face. "Tell me about your mother."

"I don't remember a lot about her," Kelly said evasively.

"Weren't you eight when she died?"

"Yes."

"That's plenty of time to make memories that stick," Ivy said, refusing to back down. "What did you do with her?"

"My mom wasn't big on movies," Kelly said, keeping her attention fixed on the television. "She loved music, though."

"What kind of music?"

"Old stuff … like this."

"Stop calling this music old," Ivy warned. "I'm in my twenties. I'm not old."

"I didn't say *you* were old," Kelly said. "I just said you liked old stuff. I'm not sure there's anything wrong with that."

"There's not."

"Anyway, my mom liked to listen to old music, and she was always trying to get me to dance," Kelly said. "I didn't have any rhythm, though, so that never went well."

"Well, at least you tried," Ivy said. "I don't have any rhythm either. Don't feel bad."

"I wonder if she saw this movie," Kelly mused.

"This movie is a classic for a reason," Ivy said. "I'm sure she did. I … ." Ivy broke off, an inner warning alarm dinging in the back of her mind. She shifted quickly, her gaze focused on the front window of the cottage. "Someone is here."

"What do you mean?" Kelly asked, furrowing her brow. "Is Jack back? Is Max here? I just love your brother."

"That's not what I mean," Ivy said, pushing herself to her feet. "Someone is outside … someone who isn't supposed to be here."

"How do you know that?" Kelly asked, her eyes shifting from hopeful to terrified in the blink of an eye. "Is it him?"

"We need to have a talk about who 'him' is," Ivy said. "I don't know who is outside. I don't even know how I know someone is out there. I just … ."

At that precise moment, Nicodemus started howling. Ivy knew the cat well enough to realize he was warning them.

Ivy reached for Kelly, her hand snaking around the girl's wrist, and then the front door exploded as someone tried to kick it in. The security chain kept it from flying completely open, but the man in the open space – his face hidden by a knit ski mask – was staring at them from the opening.

That's when Kelly started to scream, and Ivy began to panic. What was she supposed to do now?

THIRTEEN

"So, what do you like to do for fun?"

The blonde Max saddled Jack with – her name was Trina, or Tina, or something equally annoying – rubbed her fingers against Jack's hand suggestively.

"I like to solve crimes and work on my house," Jack replied drily, shifting farther away from the blonde and shooting Max a death look.

"That sounds boring," Trina said. "Do you like to dance?"

"No."

"Do you like to hike in the woods?"

"No."

"Do you like to go camping?"

"Definitely not."

Max struggled to keep himself from laughing out loud as he watched Jack try to fend off the blonde's advances. The other blonde was trying to focus his attention on her, but Max was having a better time watching Jack grapple with his handsy new friend. She kept running her fingers up and down his thigh, and Jack was close to exploding. Max was mildly curious to see what would happen when he did.

"You have to like something," Trina prodded.

"I like it when people keep their hands to themselves," Jack said pointedly, grabbing Trina's hand by the wrist and pushing it to her own lap. "Stop touching me."

Max snorted. He couldn't help himself. "So, Jack, how are you feeling about my sister now?"

"You did this on purpose," Jack charged, his tone accusatory.

"I did," Max agreed. "The grass is always greener on the other side. How does Ivy's grass look now?"

The mere mention of Ivy's name was enough to cause Jack's heart to warm. "Better than this," he said. "I ... ." The sound of his phone ringing in his pocket cut him off. Jack dug it out. "I hope this is work."

"Oh, don't say things like that," Trina said. "If you have to go to work, how am I going to get to know you?"

"You're never going to get to know me," Jack said, pressing the phone to his ear. "Keep your hands where I can see them. Hello?"

"Jack?"

"Kelly?"

Max instantly sobered, leaning forward so he could better hear Jack's end of the conversation.

"What's going on?" Jack asked.

Max watched as Jack's face drained of color.

"Kelly, listen to me," Jack said. "I'm on my way. Stay in the closet. Don't come out. Don't you dare come out of that bedroom until Max and I get there. Do you understand?"

Jack disconnected and jumped to his feet, digging a few bills out of his pocket and dumping them on the table.

"What's going on?" Max asked, following suit. He didn't like the grim set of Jack's jaw, or the worried look pinching the man's features.

"Kelly said someone broke into the house," Jack said, forcing his voice to remain even. "Ivy sent Kelly into the bedroom again while she ... we have to get out there."

"Where is Ivy? Is she okay?"

"Kelly doesn't know where Ivy is," Jack said, his voice cracking. "Whoever it is got inside of the house. That's all I know. Come on."

. . .

JACK WAS a jumble of nerves by the time they pulled into Ivy's driveway. Max was out of the truck and racing toward the gaping front door before Jack could kill his engine and follow. The short trip between his truck and Ivy's house was the longest five seconds of his life, and when he raced up the steps and into the living room, his heart lodged in his throat.

There had obviously been a struggle. The coffee table was tipped over on its side and a bowl of popcorn was upended on the floor. A vase – the one usually perched in the middle of the coffee table – was shattered into pieces against the wall next to the door, as if someone used it as a weapon. The room was otherwise empty.

"Where are they?" Max asked.

Jack pointed to the hallway wordlessly, following Max to Ivy's bedroom. The door was locked, and as Max raised his leg to kick it in, Jack stayed him with a small shake of his head.

"Kelly? It's Jack. If you can hear me, open this door."

The unmistakable sound of someone moving on the other side of the door hit Jack's ears, and when the door finally opened, Kelly's tear-streaked face popped into view. She was clutching a wriggling Nicodemus against her chest, and her eyes were so red and puffy they were almost swollen shut.

When she caught sight of the men, she threw herself at Max and started sobbing incoherently. Max did his best to calm the distraught girl while Jack strode into the bedroom and searched the room.

"Ivy sensed someone was outside before anything happened," Kelly said. "I thought she was just … screwing around. She wasn't, though. The next thing I knew someone was kicking in the door.

"The security chain held the first time," Kelly said, her tear onslaught relentless. "He just kept kicking it until it gave in, though. Ivy threw a vase at him and then attacked him. She told me to run and hide. She told me to call for help. I didn't know what else to do."

"You did the right thing," Max said, rubbing the girl's back as he lifted his terrified eyes to Jack. Kelly was safe. They were both thankful for that, but … .

"Kelly, where is Ivy?" Jack asked, his voice strangled as he fought to tamp down the irrational anger coursing through his body. "Where did she go after ... after she attacked him?"

"I don't know," Kelly wailed. "She told me to run. That's what I did. I could hear them fighting, and I think I heard Ivy cry out. I didn't hear anything after that, though. I don't know where she is."

Icy fingers wrapped around Jack's heart and squeezed as he pressed his eyes shut briefly. She had to be all right. He couldn't take it otherwise. He wrenched his eyes back open and focused on Max. "You take care of her," he said. "Call Brian and get him out here."

"Wait, I want to help you look for Ivy," Max said, trying to disengage himself from the frantic teenager.

"Ivy would want you to take care of Kelly," Jack said. "Do it. Do what I said. Don't worry. I'll find Ivy."

"What if you don't?" Max's voice was ragged as he tried to maintain an air of calm for Kelly's benefit.

"I'll find her," Jack said. "I'll find her if I have to burn this whole town down to do it."

IVY'S SHOULDER was throbbing and her heart was racing, but she fought to keep her breathing in check as she hid behind the tree.

When the man finally broke his way into the house, Ivy did the only thing she could think to do: fight. She threw her favorite vase at him, all the while urging Kelly down the hallway with Nicodemus. Once she was sure the girl was safe, Ivy unleashed days' worth of misery and anger on the intruder.

How dare anyone break into her house?

After slapping him around a little bit, the man threw her against the wall. Hard. Between the clanging in her head, and the churning in her stomach, Ivy was sure she would lose consciousness. She knew she couldn't allow that to happen, so instead of giving into the dark corners invading her mind, Ivy started yelling as the man tried to make his way down the hallway. She grabbed her cell phone off the table by the door and bolted through it, drawing the man's attention back to her as she loudly proclaimed she was calling the police.

In an effort to stop her, the intruder gave up his pursuit of Kelly and instead chased Ivy outside. This was her turf. She knew every hiding place. Instead of drawing the man farther into the woods, though, she opted to keep him close to the house as she led him on a merry chase through the trees. She knew Kelly was calling for help. She just had to hang on long enough for them to get to her.

Whoever the man was, he wasn't familiar with the intricacies of wandering through unfamiliar woods at night. He'd tripped and fallen so many times Ivy couldn't figure out how he hadn't knocked himself out yet. The unmistakable sound of a vehicle pulling into her driveway gave Ivy hope. The cavalry had arrived, although the intruder was still too close for her to yell out.

Instead of racing for safety, Ivy opted to remain in her spot. She couldn't see the man, but she could hear him. She didn't start moving until she saw a hint of black movement – running into the woods and away from her house. That's when she stumbled out of the thick foliage and back into her yard – and right into Jack's path as he desperately searched for her.

"Ivy?"

Relief washed over her, and even as she struggled to maintain her footing, she trudged toward him. "Jack."

Jack raced to her, drawing her into his arms and pulling her tightly against his chest. "I thought … you scared me."

Ivy burst into tears. She'd meant to brush everything off and pretend like someone kicking in her door didn't bother her. Despite all her strength, though, that was a feat she wasn't capable of accomplishing.

Jack held her, rubbing his hand over the back of her head as he rocked her. "It's okay. You're okay."

"Jack." Ivy couldn't say anything but his name as she buried her face into his solid chest. His arms were warm as they engulfed her, and after a few minutes, Ivy realized he was lifting her off the ground and carrying her toward the house. "I'm still capable of walking," she grumbled.

"Yeah, I know," Jack said. "I wanted to be manly and carry you, though."

"**ARE** YOU SURE YOU'RE OKAY?" Max asked, his face a mottled shade of red as he knelt down in front of Ivy and checked her arm.

"I'm fine," Ivy said. "I'm just sore."

"You didn't recognize him?" Brian asked from his spot behind the couch where his head was bent close to Jack's.

"No. He had one of those black masks on. Why do people even sell those masks? Only criminals buy them."

"I'll get to work on outlawing the masks first thing in the morning," Brian said.

"The first thing we have to get to work on is securing that door," Jack said, exerting his no-nonsense attitude. "Max, is there any wood around this place that we can use to brace it?"

"Yeah," Max said, sighing as he got to his feet. "There's some in the shed around back."

"Go see what you can find," Jack said. "And … be careful. We can't be sure this guy is really gone."

"I saw him run off into the woods," Ivy said, weary. "When he heard your truck he took off."

"Maybe he came back," Jack suggested.

"I'm too tired to argue with you Jack," Ivy said, resigned. "Wow. Those are words I never thought I'd say out loud. You win, though. He's probably out there listening to us right now."

Jack thought winning an argument with Ivy would be more thrilling. He moved over to her side and sat down next to her, carefully reaching over so he could check her shoulder. "How badly does this hurt?"

"It's fine."

Jack growled, the sound reminiscent of a bear Ivy once stumbled across while camping with her family as a child. "Nice," she said, making a face.

"Are you sure your shoulder isn't dislocated?" Jack asked, being as gentle as he could as he lifted her arm.

Ivy grimaced, but when she displayed a full range of motion, Jack dropped the arm back down.

"What do you want to do?" Brian asked.

"Well, all we can do right now is make a report," he said, lifting his eyes to Kelly's frightened face. "I'm going to stay here for the rest of the night in case our friend returns."

"You can't do that," Ivy said, instantly more alert.

"You can't stop me, honey," Jack said.

"I only have one bedroom."

"And I think Kelly should sleep in there with you," Jack said, not missing a beat. "I'll sleep on the couch."

"But . . . ."

"No buts, Ivy," Jack said, his tone firm. "You two need some sleep. You're not going to be able to get it if you don't feel safe. I'm going to be sleeping on this couch the entire night. I don't want to hear one word of argument from you."

"But . . . ."

Jack held up his index finger in warning.

"Fine," Ivy said, crossing her arms over her chest and whimpering as the pain coursed through her.

"We all need to regroup tomorrow," Jack said, his eyes thoughtful as he focused on Kelly. "For now, though, everyone needs to get some sleep. Max and I will jerry rig the door. I'm going to get a new one tomorrow. One that has a deadbolt."

"Maybe I don't want a new door," Ivy sniffed.

"Maybe you're going to shut up and do what I tell you to do for a change," Jack countered.

Ivy glared at him. "You and I are going to have words tomorrow morning."

"I can't wait."

FOURTEEN

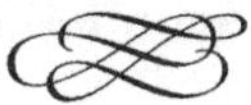

Ivy found the energy to argue for another half hour, and then she dragged Kelly to the bedroom and settled in for the night. After Max and Jack worked to brace the door, Max left Jack with a rueful smile and let Brian drive him back to the bar to reclaim his truck.

Jack didn't think he could fall asleep. He was keyed up from his Ivy search, and Max's disastrous attempt to dislodge the woman from his mind. Despite the long odds facing him, though, Jack drifted off within minutes of his head hitting the pillow.

Not long after he woke up, a shuffling sound in the quiet house dragging him from his sleep. He'd stripped out of his jeans and shirt and was only clad in his boxers, but he'd placed his gun on the coffee table just to be on the safe side. He was reaching for it when he heard her voice.

"It's just me."

Jack lifted himself up on one elbow and glanced over the arm of the couch, his eyes finding Ivy in the darkness. "What's wrong, honey?"

"I . . . ."

"You're too scared to sleep, aren't you?"

"I'm not scared," Ivy grumbled.

Jack sighed and lifted the blanket, gesturing to the spot next to him on the couch. "Come on."

"You want me to sleep on the couch with you?" Ivy was surprised.

"You're going to invade my dreams anyway," Jack said. "You might as well have a shorter route to take."

Ivy worried her bottom lip with her teeth, unsure. "Do you think that's a good idea?"

"Isn't this why you came out here?"

It was, but Ivy had no intention of admitting it. "I was just going to make some warm milk."

"Come on," Jack prodded, his voice soft. "Kelly is in the other room. I promise not to molest you when you have a guest."

Ivy wordlessly closed the distance between them and climbed on the couch, rolling to her side so her sore shoulder wasn't bearing the brunt of her weight. Jack cuddled up behind her, slipping an arm under her waist on the bottom, and the other over her waist on the top, as he pulled her close.

She smelled like peaches today. The remnants of whatever lotion she'd slathered on clinging to her skin almost a full day later. He inhaled deeply and then rested his head on the pillow next to hers. "Try to sleep, honey."

"This is a terrible idea, isn't it?"

"Crawling under a blanket and snuggling up with me? Yes, it's a terrible idea."

"Why are you letting me?" Ivy asked seriously.

"Because I can't bear the thought of letting you go right now," Jack said. "I wasn't lying when I said you scared me. I thought … I thought you sacrificed yourself for Kelly. I didn't know if I'd ever see you again. Now, go to sleep."

"I know this doesn't mean anything," Ivy said. "I'm not trying to pressure you. I'm just … ."

"Scared," Jack said. He didn't add what else he was thinking. He didn't tell her he was starting to believe that every interaction they had meant something. "I won't let anyone hurt you, Ivy. I'll be right here. Go to sleep."

"Okay," Ivy said, closing her eyes and nestling closer to him.

Jack didn't fight the feelings. He wasn't sure if he could. "Goodnight, honey."

"Goodnight." Ivy's voice was barely a murmur.

"I'll be right here," Jack whispered into her ear.

"DID YOU TWO ... you know ... do it?"

Despite her current predicament, and the fact that a masked assailant broke into Ivy's house hell bent on hurting her the night before, Kelly was bright-eyed as she stared at Jack and Ivy the next morning.

"What are you doing up so early?" Ivy asked, rubbing her eyes as she tried to get her bearings.

"It's almost ten."

Jack groaned as he shifted next to Ivy, hating the fact that he was going to have to release her in a few seconds. He hadn't slept so heavily since ... well ... since his world imploded at the end of a gun almost a year before. "I can't believe it's so late."

"You didn't answer my question," Kelly said. "Did you two do it last night?"

"No," Ivy said, pushing herself to a sitting position and lowering her feet to the ground. "Ow."

Jack reached up and rubbed her back, being careful to steer clear of her shoulder. "How much pain are you in?"

"I'm fine."

"You're like a parrot who only knows two words," Jack grumbled.

"So you didn't do it?" Kelly looked disappointed.

"No," Ivy said, making a face.

"That's too bad," Kelly said. "Max says it's coming soon. I want to see if he's always right like he says he is."

"Max is an idiot," Ivy said, struggling to her feet and almost toppling over before Jack caught her.

"Slow down, Speed Racer," he said. "You need to move slowly until your body adjusts to its new reality."

"And what reality is that?"

"The one where you're not super human."

"I need to make breakfast," Ivy said. "I promised Kelly pancakes."

"You don't have to," Kelly said. "You're in pain."

"I'm not in pain."

"Shut up, Ivy," Jack said, climbing off the couch and reaching for his shirt. He didn't miss Kelly's eyes as they latched onto the scars on his chest. He opted to ignore her overt interest. "I'm cooking breakfast."

Ivy arched an eyebrow. "You're cooking breakfast?"

"That's what I said."

"Do you know how to cook breakfast?"

"Yes," Jack said. "I've watched you do it. I believe I find whatever vegetables you have in the refrigerator, toss them in with eggs, throw it in a pan on the stove, and then bitterly complain to whoever will listen. That's the way to do it, right?"

"You're a butthead."

"You've told me," Jack said, nonplussed. "If you're a good girl, I'll let you make the coffee."

"Oh, wow, you're going to let me make the coffee in my own house? Thank you so much."

"I said you could make it if you were a good girl," Jack said. "I'm still waiting for that to happen."

"BREAKFAST IS SERVED," Jack said, sliding plates in front of Kelly and Ivy with a flourish.

"This actually looks good," Ivy said, grudgingly studying her plate and fluffing the omelet with her fork. "How did you learn to cook?"

"My mother taught me."

As Ivy and Kelly dug into their breakfasts, Jack grabbed his own plate and mug from the counter and settled between them. Everyone ate in silence for a few moments, but Jack had a direction for their morning conversation, and he was going to head that way right from the start.

"It's time you told us what's going on, Kelly."

Ivy froze, her fork halfway to her mouth. She shifted her eyes to Kelly and found the teenager's face turning from happy to sad in record time. "Jack," she warned.

Jack ignored her. "I know you don't want to talk about this Kelly. I know you're scared. It's obvious you have a right to be. We need to know what's going on if you want us to help you."

"I don't know what you're talking about," Kelly replied evasively.

"Don't do that," Jack said, fighting to keep his anger in check. "Ivy almost died trying to protect you last night. You owe us the truth."

"I haven't lied." Kelly refused to meet Jack's serious eyes.

"You haven't told us the truth either," Jack said, pinching the bridge of his nose. "I'm not trying to rush you. Ivy wants you to feel comfortable, and I applaud her for it. We need to know what's going on, though. Last night was proof that you're in danger."

"I'm not talking about this," Kelly said, dropping her fork on her plate and getting to her feet.

"Yes, you are," Jack said. "Sit down."

"No." It was the first time Kelly had stood up to any of them.

"Kelly, I want to keep you safe," Jack said. "I need your help to do it. I won't risk Ivy's life because you're too scared to tell us what's going on. You need to have faith in us. We're going out of our way to help you. Hiding whatever happened to you isn't helping anyone. In fact, it's hurting you … and it hurt Ivy pretty badly last night."

"That's pretty rich coming from you," Kelly said, lifting her chin as she defiantly met Jack's studied gaze. "Ivy said you were mad at her the other day because she invaded your privacy. Something tells me it has something to do with those scars on your chest. Do you want to tell me how you got those?"

"I … we're not talking about me," Jack replied, caught off guard by her vehemence. "I'm not the one in danger here. You're the one in danger."

"Butt out," Kelly said. "I don't want to talk about it. It's none of your business."

"Kelly, this can't go on forever," Jack said. "This isn't a game. I won't just sit idly by and watch you get hurt. I won't risk Ivy."

"Because you love her?"

Jack clenched his jaw, frustrated. "Because if something happens to her – if something happens to you – I won't be able to live with it."

"Nothing is going to happen to me," Kelly said. "Ivy is here to protect me."

"She can't save you if you don't tell us what we're fighting," Jack argued.

"Ivy can do anything," Kelly said. "I have faith." She moved away from the table. "I'm going to take a shower. Are we working in the greenhouse again today?"

Ivy nodded wordlessly, flabbergasted by Kelly's aggressive response. Jack opened his mouth to call Kelly back, but Ivy silenced him with a hand on his arm. Once Kelly disappeared down the hallway, and she was sure she'd given the girl ample time to get into the shower, Ivy turned her full attention to Jack.

"Wow."

"That's all you have to say?" Jack asked. "Why did you let her just walk away like that?"

"She obviously wasn't going to talk to you, Jack. You have to give her some space. She's not ready to tell us what happened to her."

"Ivy, this isn't a game," Jack said. "Kelly is in real danger. Someone wants her. We don't know if it's because of something she knows, or something she's done, but she's clearly on someone's radar."

"I know that," Ivy said, her voice low. "She's just ... scared. Give me a little more time."

"No."

"No?"

"I almost lost you last night," Jack said. "You almost died on me. I won't just sit back and let that happen again."

Ivy opened her mouth, her jaw working, but no sound coming out.

"Don't bother saying anything," Jack said. "I know what I said. I'm not taking it back. I don't care how ridiculous it sounds. I don't care how much you're going to fight me on this. I won't let anything happen to you. I ... can't."

Ivy's heart warmed at the admission even has her anger inflated. "Jack, I'm not asking you to go against what you know to be right. I'm just asking for a little more time. Just ... a little. Please."

She was so earnest. Her face, bare of makeup and pale after a long night, was enough to break him. "Then we have to come to an understanding," Jack said. "I'm staying here indefinitely. I won't risk you again."

"If I agree to this, will you calm down?"

"If you agree to this, I'll try to keep myself from shaking her until answers start falling out like she's a piñata," Jack replied. "I can't promise more than that. Not right now, at least."

"Okay," Ivy said. "You can stay here."

"And you're going to text me once an hour during the day so I know you're safe," Jack added.

Ivy gritted her teeth. "Fine."

"And you're going to hug me when I come back here after work today," Jack said.

"What?"

"Oh, no, I'm in the power position now, honey. You're going to hug me when I get back here tonight."

"Why?"

Jack's smile was cheeky. "Because I like it when you hug me."

Sadly, Ivy liked it, too. "Fine. Are you happy now?"

"I'm as happy as I'm going to get until this is solved," Jack said, turning his attention back to his breakfast. "Are you happy?"

"I have no idea what I am," Ivy admitted.

"Eat your breakfast."

"Don't tell me what to do."

"Eat your breakfast or I'm going to sit on your chest and feed you myself," Jack said.

"You're going to be a real pain the ass while you're staying here, aren't you?"

"You have no idea."

FIFTEEN

"How was Ivy this morning?" Brian asked Jack a few hours later, his eyes never moving from the road. The men were on their way back to Kelly's hometown, intent on talking to any and all of her friends they could find.

"She was sore."

"That's not what I meant."

"She's okay," Jack said. "She's tough."

"She's definitely tough," Brian said. "Did she sleep all right? Did she wake up with any nightmares?"

"Not that I know of." There was no way Jack was going to admit he'd wrapped his tall frame around Ivy's slighter one and held her on the couch all night. That was just begging for trouble. Now that he thought about it, Jack realized the previous evening was the first one he hadn't woken up from his own nightmare in … well … he couldn't remember the last time. He wasn't fooling himself that Ivy's presence wasn't the key change in that scenario.

"How was Kelly this morning?" Brian asked, opting to change the subject given Jack's replies.

"Belligerent."

"Do you want to expand on that?"

Jack told Brian about the breakfast exchange. When he was done, the older police officer was stunned. "I'm surprised she was so aggressive with you," he said. "That must mean she's comfortable with you."

"I'm not sure that was it," Jack said. "It wasn't that she felt so safe with me she knew I'd never hurt her. It was more like she decided she wasn't going to tell me the truth no matter what, and if I beat her to get answers, she was willing to put up with it."

"That's kind of ... chilling."

"Her face was odd," Jack admitted. "It was like she was prepared for something awful to happen, and yet even the threat of that wasn't enough to get her to tell the truth."

"What do you think she's hiding?"

"Something really bad," Jack said.

"It's summer break," Brian said, turning his attention back to the winding road in front of him. "Where do you want to look for high school kids?"

"Go to the school."

"I just told you it was summer break," Brian reminded him.

"It's also a small town," Jack said. "Most schools have basketball courts. We should be able to find some teenage boys there to start with. They'll direct us where to go after that."

"I take it you've done this before."

"Not exactly this," Jack clarified. "Teenagers are the same everywhere, though."

"Okay," Brian said. "I know where the high school is. We'll start there."

"DO YOU KNOW KELLY SISTO?" Jack asked, trying to remain casual as the teenage boys eyed him suspiciously. He remembered what it was like to be their age. Even if you weren't doing anything wrong, the arrival of police officers was still cause for concern.

"I know her." The boy, who identified himself as Kevin, was standoffish. "What did she do?"

"She didn't do anything," Jack said. "She was … injured ... over in Shadow Lake the other day. We're trying to find out who hurt her."

"Why don't you just ask her?" another boy, this one named Mitch, asked.

"She's having some issues right now," Jack said honestly. "She's scared to tell us what happened to her. That's why we're here."

"We didn't do anything to her," Kevin said quickly.

"I know that," Jack said. "We don't think you did. I promise. We're just trying to find out who she hung around with."

"Did she have any good friends?" Brian asked.

"She was kind of a loner," Mitch said. "She had a few friends, but I wouldn't really call them close friends. I think she was embarrassed because of her home situation."

"What do you know about that?" Jack asked.

"I know that her foster parents never came to school conferences, or games, or parents' night. I can't ever remember seeing her with them other than once or twice at the grocery store. It was more like she didn't have parents."

"I think she was kind of on her own," Kevin said.

"To your knowledge, did she ever get in any trouble?"

"No," Kevin said. "She was one of those girls who sat at the end of the bleachers all by herself during a game. She never even watched it. She always had her nose stuck in a book."

"Did she have any boyfriends?" Brian asked, not missing the quick look Mitch and Kevin exchanged.

"I never saw her with anyone," Mitch replied carefully.

"You heard rumors, though, didn't you?" Jack pressed.

"Some of the girls spread rumors about her," Kevin said. "I'm not sure if they were true or not."

"We're not looking to shoot the messenger."

"Kayla Clayvin told a few people that Kelly supposedly had an older boyfriend and they were … doing it."

"How old?" Jack asked.

"Old enough that she got called into the guidance counselor's office to talk about it," Kevin said. "I have no idea what happened in there, but whatever it was, Kelly had to spend a lot of time in the office."

"And you have no idea who this supposed boyfriend was?" Jack asked.

"None, man," Mitch said. "She was a total loner. She never talked to us."

"Do you think she was shy, or do you think something else was going on?" Brian asked.

"I think that Kelly was just marking time," Mitch said. "Once she turned eighteen, she knew she was going to be turned out on the street. That's the way the system works. I heard her talking about it one day.

"She knew she wasn't going to college, and she knew her grades didn't matter, so she only kept them up to make sure her foster parents didn't come down on her," he continued. "She was making plans to find a restaurant job over the summer because she pretty much figured that was her future."

The statement made Jack inexplicably sad. "Tell me about this guidance counselor. What's his name?"

"Mr. Thorpe."

"Does he have a first name?" Jack asked.

"Oh, yeah, Gil."

"I don't suppose you know where he lives, do you?" Brian asked.

Mitch shrugged. "He lives on the same street as my grandparents."

Jack and Brian exchanged a look. They both knew where their next stop would be.

GIL THORPE WAS in his late thirties, and he dressed like he'd just stepped off of the pages of a J.Crew catalog. His khakis were pressed and pristine. His loafers had actual pennies in them. His polo shirt looked like it hadn't gone through the wash yet. He clearly took pride in his appearance, even though there was nothing about him that stood out.

He also seemed genuinely shocked to hear about Kelly's situation.

"I don't know what to say," he said, handing Jack and Brian bottles of water as he settled on the couch across from them. "I had no idea Kelly was even missing, let alone ... any of that."

"That doesn't surprise me," Jack said. "Her foster parents didn't know she was missing until we told them either."

"Well, I wish I could say that was out of character for them, but the Gideons are ... limited ... in the way they deal with Kelly," Gil said. "When Kelly first started having trouble, I thought they would be helpful in my efforts to rein her in. I was wrong."

"What kind of trouble are we talking about?" Brian asked.

"I want to start by saying that I think Kelly is a gifted student," Gil said. "She's been overlooked her whole life because no one took the time to realize how smart she is. Now, I'm not casting aspersions on the foster care system. I know caseworkers are busy, and I know it's impossible for them to take special interest in any one child.

"Kelly was still overlooked," he said. "Had someone spent more time with her when she was younger, she might have been put in the gifted and talented classes, and her future might be vastly different."

"So, you're saying she's smart," Jack said.

"She's very smart," Gil said. "She reads faster than just about any student I've ever encountered, and she truly loves books. She does lag a little in science and math, but I think it's because she doesn't apply herself. She's learned she doesn't have to excel at anything because no one cares enough to make her. She does just enough to get by, and she puts minimal effort in to do that."

"What do you know about her friends?" Brian asked.

"As far as I can tell, she doesn't have any," Gil said. "I'm not going to pretend I watch her in the lunchroom or anything, but Kelly is one of those kids who isolates herself. I think she's embarrassed by her circumstances so she doesn't want anyone to get close enough to ask about them."

"Her foster parents insinuated she had friends," Jack said.

"You also said her foster parents had no idea where she was spending her nights or where she was from day to day," Gil said. "I would be surprised if those people even knew her middle name. Well, scratch that, if her middle name appeared on the checks from the state, then they might've known it."

Jack grimaced. "What about boyfriends? The boys on the basketball court said there was a rumor she was dating an older boy."

"That's the first I'm hearing about that," Gil said.

"They said that's why she was called to your office for meetings," Brian said.

Gil chuckled. "I'm sure someone made that up just so the other kids would have something to gossip about," he said. "Kelly was called into my office for regular meetings for … behavioral issues."

"Like?"

"I'm not sure how much I should tell you," Gil admitted. "I'm not a licensed therapist, but my sessions with these kids are supposed to be private."

"We need information," Jack said. "Kelly is in danger."

"I guess that trumps everything else," Gil said, rubbing his chin thoughtfully. "Kelly was brought to my attention because two different teachers said she was lying. At first they were small lies about why she didn't finish her homework … stuff like her computer died, or one of her foster siblings spilled milk on it. Then she started telling bigger lies."

"Can you give us some examples?" Brian asked.

"Sure," Gil said. "She told the lunch lady that her foster parents died and she was raising her foster siblings on her own. She told the librarian that aliens were abducting her from her bed at night so they could do experiments on her. She told the custodian that she was being stalked by a government agency who implanted a chip in her brain."

Jack was floored. She'd never mentioned any of those things to him, and he was fairly certain Max and Ivy would've told him if she'd said anything of the sort to them. "Why do you think she did that?"

"I think she's starved for attention," Gil said. "It's not uncommon with kids in similar circumstances. When they feel everyone has forgotten them, they go out of their way to make sure someone will remember them – even if it's because they lie."

"How were you treating Kelly?"

"Technically, I'm not treating her," Gil said. "I don't have the authority. Basically, I just called her into my office twice a week and let her talk. She just wanted attention, so I let her talk to me as much as she wanted. Most of it was mundane, but I think the human contact was the most important thing."

"And you're sure you don't know anything about an older boyfriend, right?" Jack asked.

"I'm sure."

Jack and Brian got to their feet, extending their hands in turn to Gil.

"Thanks for talking to us," Jack said.

"I just hope I helped."

"You gave us … a lot to think about," Jack said.

"I do have a question," Gil said as he led them to the door. "What's going to happen to Kelly now?"

"We're not sure yet," Brian said. "I can tell you she will not be returning to the Gideons. I believe the state is looking for a new foster family, but she's in limbo right now."

"Where is she staying?"

"At a safe place in Shadow Lake," Jack said.

"I hope you find out what happened to her," Gil said. "The girl has already been through so much. I fear something like this might break her."

"She's strong," Jack said. "We're doing everything in our power to see that she remains that way."

"That's good," Gil said. "We need more police officers like you. God bless you."

Jack's cheeks burned under the praise. "Um … thanks."

"Thank you for your time," Brian said. "We might stop by to talk again if something comes up."

"Stop in whenever you want," Gil said. "If you feel like it might help for me to talk to Kelly, don't hesitate to ask."

"We'll consider it."

SIXTEEN

"Where are we going?" Kelly asked, following Ivy into the woods on the far side of her property. "I thought we were going back to the greenhouse after lunch."

"We're going for a walk," Ivy said. "We've done enough work for one day."

"But … why are we going into the woods?" Kelly was nervous. She had an unfortunate habit of wringing her hands when she didn't know what else to do with them. She wasn't prone to excited utterances and gestures. Ivy had a feeling it was because she went out of her way to remain calm since she was always in someone else's house, but she wanted to test the theory further before making up her mind.

"I happen to love the woods," Ivy said. "I find them … relaxing."

"But … ." Kelly broke off, biting her lower lip.

Ivy slowed her forward momentum. "But what?"

"Aren't you afraid?"

"What would I be afraid of?"

"The man who broke into your house last night." Kelly's voice was barely a whisper.

"I thought you didn't want to talk about him."

"I don't."

"I'm not frightened of these woods," Ivy said, choosing her words carefully. "I grew up in these woods. I daydreamed in these woods. I played games with Max in these woods. These woods are magic. No one can ever take that away from me."

"Magic?" Kelly looked both surprised and hopeful.

"There are all different kinds of magic," Ivy said. "Some you can see, and some you can feel. I'm going to take you to a place where you can do both."

"And we'll be safe?"

"We'll be safe," Ivy said. "I promised to keep you safe. I plan on keeping that promise."

"What if he is out here?" Kelly asked, her fingers shaking.

"I don't think he would risk coming out here when the sun is still out," Ivy said. "You don't have to worry about him coming back tonight either. Jack will be back before the sun sets. He's staying with us again."

"I thought he was angry with me."

"Jack is frustrated," Ivy said. "He's dealing with a few things of his own, and he's trying to keep us safe. He's got a lot on his plate."

"Why won't he talk about those scars on his chest?" Kelly asked.

"Because he's not ready to do it yet," Ivy replied. "You shouldn't have brought them up. You more than anyone should realize that Jack needs to deal with his wounds on his own timetable. You don't want to be pushed, so why did you think it was all right to push Jack?"

"I didn't mean to hurt him," Kelly said, her green eyes wide as they landed on Ivy's conflicted blue ones. "I really didn't. I like Jack."

"Jack has a job to do," Ivy said. "He's a good man. He wants to help you. Heck, Jack is the type of man who will die to protect you. He still deserves his own secrets."

"I'll apologize," Kelly said, her voice low.

"You will," Ivy agreed. "When Jack presses you on what happened, he's not trying to hurt you. He's trying to help you. I understand you don't want to talk about it. I understand something truly terrible happened to you. I don't understand why you're protecting the man who hurt you, though."

"That's not what I'm doing," Kelly said, her knuckles whitening under the exertion she was using to hold her hands in place.

"Then what are you doing?"

"I don't want to think about it," Kelly said. "Can't you understand that?"

"I can."

"Can't you accept it and let it go?"

"No," Ivy said. "What I can do is promise to let it go for the next few hours, though. I want to take you to a special place. I'm hoping it will help you as much as it helped me."

"WHAT DO YOU THINK?" Jack asked from the passenger seat of Brian's car as they headed back toward Shadow Lake.

"I think Kelly has lived a very sad life," Brian said.

"If the guidance counselor is right, and he seemed pretty sincere, Kelly is one of those kids who is smarter than anyone around her realizes," Jack said. "She's probably bored in class, and disinterested in life outside of it."

"What do you think about the boyfriend?"

"Just because she didn't own up to having an older boyfriend to Thorpe, that doesn't mean he doesn't exist," Jack said. "High school kids are all over the place with the gossip, but a lot of times it does stem from something real. They might not have all the details right, but I'm betting they have some of them right."

"Thorpe has been trying to help Kelly find focus in her life," Brian said. "If he's right about the lying … ."

"I know what you're thinking," Jack said. "Even if Kelly showed up in Ivy's greenhouse looking for attention, that doesn't explain the guy who tried to break into Ivy's house. Ivy wasn't thrown into the wall by a lie."

"That's true," Brian said. "What if Kelly knows something about someone and they're desperate to shut her up? She has a reputation as a liar, but someone might be scared that she'll find the right set of ears and be vindicated for telling the truth."

"That would explain why Kelly is so frightened," Jack said. "We have no way of knowing what she knows until she tells us, though."

"And she's still refusing to talk about it," Brian mused. "How long do you think that will last?"

"As long as Ivy keeps enabling her."

"Ivy is going to protect that girl with every ounce of strength she has," Brian said. "You might want to pick a different battle."

"Ivy and I have come to an understanding," Jack said. "I'm going to let her drag the truth out of Kelly at her own pace as long as she lets me stay at her house to make sure they're safe after dark."

"Oh, well, that's convenient," Brian said, his smirk wry.

"I'm sleeping on the couch," Jack said, not bothering to admit he'd shared it with a guest the previous evening.

"I didn't say you weren't," Brian said. "That's a small cottage for two big personalities, though."

"We'll be fine," Jack said. "Ivy is scared, too. She doesn't want to admit it, but she is."

"And you're going to keep her safe, aren't you?"

"Even if it kills me," Jack confirmed.

"WHAT IS THIS PLACE?" Kelly's eyes were as wide as saucers as she looked around Ivy's fairy ring with unabashed delight. The round circle of mushrooms was naturally occurring, and it just happened to ring a tree that was so old it appeared to have a wizened face.

"It's called a fairy ring," Ivy said, smiling. This was her favorite place on Earth. Whenever she visited, she believed all things were possible.

"What is it, though?"

"Well, it depends on what you believe," Ivy said. "Fairy rings pop up in folklore throughout time. Some people think that fairy rings are made by dragon tails. Some people believe that fairy rings are where the Devil goes to churn milk."

Kelly giggled as she rolled her eyes. "Do you expect me to believe that?"

"I didn't say I believed it," Ivy clarified. "I was just telling you what other people believe. Some people also believe they're circles where witches cast spells."

Kelly stilled. "Are you a witch?"

"Did you hear someone refer to me as one?" Ivy asked.

"No, but I heard you and Jack arguing about sharing dreams yesterday," Kelly replied. "I … um … you admitted to walking in his dreams. I don't know what that means, but I think that's why Jack was so upset the other day."

"Technically, I identify myself as Wiccan sometimes," Ivy said. "That's a belief system, though. I don't call myself a witch. I don't believe I can fly on a broom, or curse people into doing what I want. I do believe in magic, though."

"Does that include walking in Jack's dreams?"

"I don't know what's going on with Jack's dreams," Ivy admitted. "It's never happened to me before."

"Can you do it because you're a witch?" Kelly was genuinely curious.

"If you're asking me if I believe I have magical powers, the answer is no," Ivy said. "I am open to the possibility of different forms of earth magic, though. I believe that there is power in words, and beliefs. Even though I identify myself as Wiccan, I think it's more apt to say that I'm a spiritual naturalist.

"Before you ask the obvious next question, that means I love nature," she continued. "I believe that magic stems from nature, although there are a lot of different types of magic."

"Do you believe in God?" Kelly asked.

That was a tricky question. Ivy asked it of herself numerous times. The simple answer was: She didn't know. "I believe in a lot of things. I don't necessarily believe it matters what your faith is as long as you believe in yourself. What do you believe in?"

"I don't believe in anything," Kelly said matter-of-factly. "My foster parents made me go to church sometimes, but I don't believe in God."

"Why not?"

"Because I can't believe in any benevolent God who would take my parents away from me and thrust me into this life," Kelly said. "If there is a God, he's not one I would ever want to know."

"Bad things happen all the time, Kelly," Ivy said. "No one can control everything. What happened to you is terrible. What happened to your parents is terrible. You can't go back in time and change it, though."

"I keep feeling like I'm living someone else's life," Kelly said. "I can't help but feel that this isn't the life I was supposed to live."

"What life do you think you were supposed to live?"

"I was supposed to grow up in the same house with my mother, father, and brother," Kelly said. "I was supposed to get Christmases with them. They were all supposed to be there when I graduated from high school. My father was supposed to walk me down the aisle. My brother was supposed to tease me, like Max teases you."

This was the first time Ivy heard mention of a brother. "I didn't know you had a brother."

"He was older than me," Kelly said. "He was a teenager when my parents died. They tried to keep us together, but Jordan was older so he went to a big place that had a lot of teenagers, and I went to a family who said they were looking to adopt a child."

"What happened then?"

"They kept me for nine months, and then they got offered a baby," Kelly said. "They said they wanted to keep us both, but it was just too much work, and I got sent back into the system the day they got their baby girl."

Ivy pressed her eyes shut, horrified. "I don't know what to say to that," she said. "You know you didn't do anything wrong, right?"

"No one wants to make me part of their family," Kelly said. "That was a valuable lesson for me. That's when I realized I was on my own. I'm okay with that. I'll be fine."

"I don't think you believe that," Ivy said. "You want a family. I understand that. As frustrating as my family is, I wouldn't trade them for the world. You can still make a family of your own."

"Maybe some day," Kelly said. "Not now, though."

"Come with me." Ivy held her hand out, watching as Kelly wordlessly took it. Then she led the teenager into the middle of the fairy ring and directed her to sit. Once they were both settled, Ivy drew Kelly's hands into hers. "Close your eyes."

"What are we going to do?" Kelly asked, nervously glancing around.

"We're going to let all of the hurt go," Ivy said. "Close your eyes and breathe. Just breathe. Push everything out of your mind. Don't think about what happened to you. Don't think about what's going to happen next. Just focus on the now."

"And then what?"

"And then we'll see where the day takes us," Ivy said.

SEVENTEEN

Kelly's face was still streaked with drying tears as Ivy led her out of the woods two hours later. She had no idea what the girl saw – or felt – but she couldn't help but hope the teenager finally managed to put some of the pain behind her.

Ivy knew there was a lot more healing to go, though.

Broad male shoulders met Ivy's gaze as she rounded the corner of her house, and for a moment she was taken aback thinking someone had come for Kelly. When the man turned, though, Ivy was relieved to find Max's face staring back at her.

"Where were you?" Max asked.

"We took a walk," Ivy said. "What are you doing here?"

"I just had your new door installed," he said. "Come look."

Ivy trudged to the front of the house, not missing Max's face as he studied Kelly's drawn features. He wisely kept his mouth shut and directed Ivy toward the painted metal monstrosity he was so proud of. "This is ugly."

"I'll paint it a different color this weekend," Max said. "You can live with it for now. No one is getting through this door. It has a deadbolt, and I installed a new security chain."

"What color are you going to paint it?" Ivy asked.

"Why is it that you fixate on the stupid stuff?" Max asked.

"Why is it that you won't tell me what color you're going to paint this door?"

"I'm going to paint it pink, just like your hair."

"Pink is good for hair," Ivy said. "It's not good for a door, though."

"Fine. What color do you want me to paint it?"

"Green."

"Fine. I'll paint it green."

"I want you to touch up the trim while you're at it," Ivy said, studying the splintered wood in the doorjamb. "I don't like it like this. It makes me unhappy."

"Well, we can't have that," Max said, rolling his eyes until they landed on Kelly. "What do you think? Is this a fancy door, or what?"

"It looks strong," Kelly said, rubbing her fingertips over the metal. "No one can get in, right?"

"No one can get in," Max reassured her.

"Jack will be sleeping on the couch, too," Ivy reminded her. "You'll be safe."

"Okay," Kelly said. "I'm … um … going to go and wash my face in the bathroom. Is that okay?"

"Take your time," Ivy said. "We'll decide what we want for dinner when you're done."

Kelly forced a wan smile. "Thank you … for everything."

"Don't mention it," Ivy said.

Once Kelly was gone, Max turned to Ivy with an arched eyebrow. "Do you want to tell me what that was all about?"

"I took her out to the fairy ring."

"Did you beat her while you were out there?"

Ivy smacked his arm. "Of course not. Do you have to be such a … ?"

"Great brother?"

"I was going to say rampant pain in my ass," Ivy countered.

"You say tomato," Max teased.

Ivy's face was serious as she studied him for a moment, and then –

without warning – she threw her arms around his neck. Max was surprised by the gesture, and he hugged her back wordlessly.

"Thank you for being such a good brother," Ivy said. "I know I don't tell you how much I love you enough."

"I know you love me," Max said, rubbing her back. "I love you, too. Do you want to tell me what this is about?"

Ivy told Max about her afternoon with Kelly. When she was done, Max was angry. "I can't believe people would just trade her in for a baby."

"It's horrible," Ivy said. "I never realized how lucky we were to have Mom and Dad until now. I mean, in the back of my mind I knew they were great parents, but we had a great childhood."

"We did," Max agreed, releasing Ivy as she took a step back. "You look tired."

"It's been a long couple of days," Ivy conceded.

"I have an idea," Max said. "Why don't you let me take Kelly for the rest of the afternoon? I'll show her around town. I'll take her to dinner. That will give you some time to yourself."

"I can't ask you to do that."

"You didn't ask," Max said. "I volunteered. I like her. It might do you two some good to be apart for a little bit."

"But … ."

"Go and see Aunt Felicity," Max prodded. "You're overwhelmed. She'll help you … clear your channels, or whatever it is the two of you do together."

"We usually gossip about you," Ivy said.

"Well, do that then," Max said, winking. "I promise I won't let Kelly out of my sight. I'll make sure she has fun."

"Thank you," Ivy said, hugging him again.

"You don't have to thank me for loving you," Max said. "Even though I wanted to trade you for Matchbox cars when you were little, I've always wanted to take care of you."

. . .

FELICITY GOODINGS WAS Luna Morgan's sister and an avowed witch. Unlike Ivy, who balked at identifying herself in such a way on most days, Felicity was more than happy to tell anyone who would listen that she was in tune with otherworldly spirits. Since she owned a magic shop, Ivy knew her aunt did part of it for show. She was also blessed with other gifts, though.

"Hello, my darling," Felicity said, drawing Ivy in for a hug when she walked through the door of her store. "I haven't seen or heard from you in days. I was starting to worry."

"I'm okay," Ivy said, hoisting herself up on one of the stools next to the counter. "How are you?"

"I'm fine," Felicity said, pushing Ivy's hair out of her face so she could study her more closely. "You look exhausted. Your aura is … scattered."

"I hate it when you do that," Ivy said. "Just because you can see auras, that doesn't mean you should comment on them."

"If you would open yourself up to other things, I'm going to bet you could see auras, too," Felicity said. "You're too stubborn to let anyone – or anything, for that matter – take control of you. You're the most obstinate witch I know."

"Well, I can't see auras," Ivy said. "I have been doing a little dream walking, though."

Felicity stilled. "Really? Wow. I've never been able to do that. I always thought it would be fun."

"Well, it's not," Ivy said. She told her aunt about Jack's dreams, refusing to go into too much detail about his past because she didn't want to betray him. When she was done, Felicity was smiling. "That's not the reaction I was expecting."

"I'm just happy for you," Felicity said.

"Because I'm invading Jack's dreams?"

"Because you've found your match," Felicity said.

"Oh, don't go there," Ivy said. "You know very well that Jack is not interested in a relationship."

"He's probably still not interested in a relationship," Felicity said. "That's what he's telling himself, at least. His head is out of the relationship game. His heart has been spoken for since the moment he saw you, though."

"You've always been a romantic at heart," Ivy said. "It's annoying."

Felicity smirked. "Ivy, you know very well that Jack is calling for you in his dreams for a reason," she said. "He doesn't want to go through whatever he keeps going through alone. He's not calling to anyone else to help him. He's calling to you."

"I can't help him," Ivy said. "I can't stop what's going to happen to him in that dream. He knows it, and I know it, too."

"You don't have to stop what happened to him," Felicity said. "It already happened. You won't solve anything by stopping it. You have to show Jack how to change his surroundings. You have to show him how to hope."

"How do I do that?"

"You've already done it," Felicity said, her eyes twinkling. "You've already changed the course of his life. You can't change his past, but you can change his dreams."

"How?"

"That's something you're going to have to figure out on your own," Felicity said. "Come over here. I want to do a reading on you." She gestured toward the small bistro table in the corner where she gave customers tarot card readings.

"I don't need a reading," Ivy grumbled.

"I want to give you one," Felicity said, her voice firm. "Don't make me wrestle you down and do it. I'm still strong enough to take you."

Since her aunt was in her mid-fifties, Ivy wasn't so sure, although it wasn't something she wanted to gamble on. She didn't think her ego could take a loss. She sighed and moved over to the table. "Has Mom told you what else is going on in my life?"

"She's told me about Kelly," Felicity said. "I'd like to meet her."

"I'm not comfortable bringing her over here," Ivy said. "I don't have a problem with you seeing her. In fact, I think it might do her some good. She's … struggling. You have to come to us, though."

"I haven't been to Shadow Lake since last fall," Felicity said. "I'm sure I can schedule a visit. Tell me about her."

"She's been abused," Ivy said. "She has bruises on her arms, and when I first found her, she had a bad reaction to men. To be fair, though, her reaction to me wasn't great in those first few moments."

"What has she told you?" Felicity asked, holding the tarot cards out so Ivy could cut them.

"Not much," Ivy said, cutting the cards and handing them back to her aunt. "She's a foster child. Her foster parents were in it for the money, not for guidance. Her parents died when she was eight, and since her brother was a teenager, they separated them.

"She was initially placed with a family who intended to adopt her, but they gave her back when a baby became available," she continued.

Felicity made a small growling noise in the back of her throat.

"I know. It's awful," Ivy said. "She's convinced herself that she's living someone else's life and she should be enjoying a happily ever after with her family. She won't tell us what happened to her. Jack and Brian have been trying to track down leads, but they're ... caught ... because Kelly won't tell them what happened."

"Someone broke into your house," Felicity said.

"How do you know that?" Ivy was surprised.

"Your mother told me," Felicity replied. "She's angry you didn't tell her, by the way. I don't think she wants to push the matter until Kelly is more settled, though, so you have that going for you."

"Max told her, didn't he?" All the love she'd been feeling for her brother evaporated. "I'm going to beat the crap out of him."

"Max loves you," Felicity said, arranging the cards on the table. "He always does what he thinks is right where you're concerned. You know that. You're not really angry with him."

"Oh, I'm angry with him."

"You are not," Felicity said. "You're actually feeling warm and fuzzy where Max is concerned because you realize what your life would be like without your family. You're putting yourself in Kelly's shoes and wondering what would've happened to you if Luna and Michael died while you were young."

"I ... how did you know that?"

"A young girl from a loving family, an older brother ... it doesn't take a lot to figure out where your head is sometimes," Felicity said. "You wouldn't have been put in the system, though. You and Max would've come to stay with me. You know that, right?"

"I know," Ivy said. "I still can't help seeing the parallels."

"There are no parallels other than the size of Kelly's family," Felicity said. "No matter what Kelly is feeling right now, she does have someone fighting for her. Several someones, if I'm not missing my guess. Where is she right now?"

"Max is spending the day with her."

"And Jack is sleeping on your couch to keep you safe," Felicity added.

"How do you know that? Oh, man, I'm going to kill Max."

Felicity chuckled. "Your brother is a fine man," she said. "One day, when he gets over his own good looks, he's going to find someone to make his own family with. He's going to be a wonderful father."

"Do you really think he's ever going to get over his looks?" Ivy asked.

"Yes," Felicity said. "It's not going to happen soon, though. You're going to have to put up with a few more years of his hound dog ways."

"Hound dog ways?" Ivy arched an eyebrow.

"I love your brother beyond reason," Felicity said. "He's still a hound dog."

Ivy couldn't argue, so she reclined in the chair and watched Felicity study the cards. After a moment, Ivy realized her aunt was being unusually quiet. Felicity often insisted on reading Ivy's cards, and she happily told Ivy she was destined for greatness – and a happily ever after. Felicity didn't look bubbly now.

"What do you see?" Ivy asked.

"I … nothing."

"Don't lie," Ivy said. "I can tell when you're lying. Tell me."

"You're in trouble," Felicity said, raising her patient eyes up to Ivy's clouded set. "You're in big trouble, dear."

Ivy wasn't sure she believed in tarot readings, but her aunt would never tell her something she didn't have faith in herself. "What about Kelly? Can you see her?"

"Your fates are linked," Felicity said. "Your future used to be clear and precise. Now I just see darkness."

"Does that mean I'm going to die?"

"I don't know," Felicity said. "I think it's more likely that your fate isn't set right now. You have to find whoever is causing the darkness."

"Meaning I have to get Kelly to talk," Ivy said.

"I don't know what all of this means, Ivy," Felicity said. "I do know you don't have a lot of time. Don't take unnecessary risks. Don't go off by yourself. Do whatever you have to do to get Kelly to talk."

"What about Jack? Do you see him?"

"Jack is your shadow now," Felicity said. "You won't be able to shake him. Your hearts are entwined. There's no going back, no matter what either of you say you want. That won't be settled right away."

"Is Jack in danger if he stays at my house?"

"Jack is your link to salvation," Felicity said. "Don't cut that link. You may think you're doing the best thing for both of you, but if you die, Jack will be as good as dead, too."

"You're saying we have to save Kelly to save ourselves, aren't you?"

"I'm saying all three of you need to survive to thrive," Felicity said. "Kelly can still have her own happily ever after. It won't be the same as she envisioned as a child, but that doesn't mean it won't be great."

"What do I do?" Ivy asked, her mouth dry.

"Trust Jack."

"I do."

"He trusts you, too," Felicity said. "Work together. That's going to be key."

"Are you telling me to stop fighting with him?"

Despite the surreal nature of their situation, Felicity chuckled. "Never stop fighting with him," she said. "He likes it. You like it, too."

"I do not," Ivy protested.

"Oh, don't lie to your aunt," Felicity said. "The cards won't let you."

"This is just crap," Ivy said, crossing her arms over her chest. "How do I know you're not making this up just so you can push us together?"

"Because I would never play games with your future," Felicity said, her eyes serious.

Ivy knew that was true. "How long do I have to get Kelly to talk?"

"Don't push her," Felicity warned, turning her attention back to the cards. "Don't let her push you away either. You'll know when the time is right."

Ivy could only hope her beloved aunt was right.

EIGHTEEN

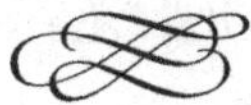

Jack was waiting on Ivy's front porch when she pulled into her driveway an hour later. The sun was still up, but it was starting to make its inevitable dip into the horizon, and under the muted light, Jack's handsome face looked magnificent.

Ivy's heart stuttered when she saw him get to his feet and descend the stairs.

"Where ... ?"

Jack didn't get a chance to finish his statement, because Ivy was on him – her arms around his waist – before he could. He pulled her close, wrapping her tight and relishing the way she folded her face into the hollow between his neck and shoulder. "What's wrong, honey?"

"Nothing is wrong," Ivy said. "I promised to greet you with a hug. That's all this is."

Jack chuckled as he rubbed his hand up and down her back. He didn't believe her. "Where have you been?"

"I was over with Aunt Felicity," Ivy said. "Max thought I needed a little time to myself, but I wanted to see her. I'm still not sure why – and now I wish I hadn't gone over there."

That was a lot for Jack to wrap his mind around. He wasn't sure which place he wanted to start. He opted for the easiest question. "Where is Kelly?"

"Max took her for the afternoon," Ivy said. "He said he was going to take her to dinner, too, so we don't have to worry about that."

"That was nice of him," Jack said, rubbing his cheek against Ivy's forehead. "You smell like limes and coconut today."

"What?"

"You smell different every day," he said. "I like to try and guess what scents you're wearing."

"Oh. I have a lot of different lotions. I just pick whichever one calls to me that particular day."

"I like it," Jack said, inhaling again. "You always smell like something I want to eat."

Ivy's face flushed. "Um … ."

"That came out dirtier than I initially envisioned," Jack said, smirking. "I just meant that you smell really good."

"Thank you … I think."

Jack's chest rumbled with his laughter. "Tell me what has you upset," he said. "Why do you wish you hadn't gone over to Felicity's?"

"I don't want to tell you," Ivy admitted. "You're going to think I'm crazy."

"I promise I won't think you're crazy."

"You can't keep that promise," Ivy said. "We both know that."

"Well, I guess it's good that I like you however I can get you," Jack said. "That includes crazy. Tell me."

Ivy told Jack about Felicity's reading, internally thanking the stars that were readying to pop up in the sky that he couldn't see her face because it was still buried in his chest. When she was done, she waited for him to laugh at her … or call her a liar … or walk away without saying another word. He didn't do any of those things.

"She thinks you're in danger? How can we change that?"

Ivy was surprised, and when she got up the courage to pull her face back far enough to lift her chin and study him, she found Jack's face to be serious but free of recrimination. "Aren't you going to tell me I'm crazy?"

"No. I want you tell me how to keep you safe."

"We have to get Kelly to talk," Ivy said. "We can't push her, though. I know you want to, but that's going to do more harm than good."

"We have to do something," Jack said, cupping the back of Ivy's head so he could stare soulfully into her eyes. "I can't go through life not seeing your face."

"Don't you dare kiss me," Ivy warned.

"I wouldn't dream of it."

"You look like you want to."

"Oh, I want to," Jack said. "I'm not going to, though. Not right now, at least."

"What are you going to do?"

Jack smiled and dropped his hands to hers, clasping them both. "I'm going to take you for a walk."

"You are?"

"We have a few things to talk about," Jack said. "I don't want to risk Kelly overhearing us."

"What happens when Max brings her back and we're not here?"

"Max is a big boy," Jack said. "He's smart enough to wait for us. We're not going to be gone for too long."

Ivy slipped her hand into Jack's and let him lead her toward the trees. He picked a slow pace, one that would allow them to talk without losing breath – or the closeness their linked fingers granted them.

"Tell me about your day," Ivy said.

Jack did as instructed, leaving nothing out. When he was done, Ivy was at a loss for words so Jack opted to fill the silence himself. "Can we go to your fairy ring?"

Ivy nodded. "I … you don't have to ask that. You're always welcome."

"That's your private place," Jack said. "I would never not ask."

"Do you remember where it is?"

"It's seared into my memory, honey," he said. "I could never forget trying to find it in the dark when Heath was chasing you." Jack was referring to an incident a few weeks before when a murderer stalked

Ivy through the woods in an attempt to kill her and throw suspicion on someone else. "I was terrified I wouldn't get to you in time. Then, when I found you, the problem was already taken care of. You'd saved yourself."

"I knew you would find me," Ivy said. "For some reason, I've had faith in you since the moment I met you."

"You hated me when you first met me."

"The first moment I saw you I thought you were the handsomest man I'd ever laid eyes on," Ivy said. "Then you opened your mouth and irritated the crap out of me."

Jack snorted. "The first moment I saw you I thought I'd died and gone to Heaven," he said. "Then you opened your mouth and I reconsidered and thought I'd gone to Hell."

"You're not being very charming," Ivy chided.

"I didn't know that was the game we were playing," Jack said. "If it's any consolation, even though you drove me crazy, I still wanted to kiss you senseless."

"Why are you telling me this?"

"I have no idea," Jack said. "I can't seem to stop myself from thinking about you. I can't seem to stop myself from dreaming about you. I can't seem to make myself stay away from you."

"I . . . ."

"We're not going to talk about this right now," Jack said. "Don't worry, we're going to talk about it. I don't want Kelly's plight hanging over us when we do, though. For now, we're just going to take a walk and pretend that this particular conversation isn't looming large."

"Okay."

"Okay?"

"I'm not in the mood to fight either," Ivy said, resting her head against Jack's shoulder as he crested the hill and her fairy ring came into view. "Here we are."

"Here we are," Jack agreed, releasing her hand and slipping his arm around her waist.

"So, what do you want to talk about?"

"Kelly," Jack said. "I want to talk about how we're going to handle her. When I say talk, that's what I mean. There will be no yelling. You can't yell here. It will ruin the magic."

"Is that why you brought me here?" Ivy asked suspiciously.

"I brought you here because I love looking at this place," Jack replied. "Even more than that, though, I love looking at you when you're in this place."

"That's kind of a schmaltzy sentiment," Ivy said.

"I'm feeling kind of schmaltzy tonight."

"Okay, what are we going to do about Kelly?"

"We need to find out about this supposed older boyfriend," Jack said. "If he's real, he could be our suspect. If he's not, she's hiding something else."

"She's never mentioned anything about a boyfriend," Ivy said. "I know that doesn't technically mean anything significant, but she's let other things slip when her guard is down."

"Like?"

"Like she told me today that she was separated from her brother after her parents died," Ivy said. "She'd never mentioned the brother before, and I think it bothers her more than she's letting on that she hasn't seen him since she was eight."

"I don't remember seeing anything about a brother in her file," Jack mused. "I'll take another look tomorrow morning."

Ivy lifted her head. "Do you think you can find him?"

"I don't see why I can't try," Jack said. "He would be an adult now, and while he's probably not in a position to help her, he might want to see her. That might be something that could jar Kelly into telling us what happened."

"She also told me she was going to be adopted by another couple," Ivy said. "She was with them for nine months, and then the state offered them a baby so they sent her back."

"That's pretty … horrible," Jack said. "No wonder she has trouble trusting people. The first people she trusted after losing her parents betrayed her. They made her feel like she was nothing."

"I think she stopped looking at her foster families as anything other than a place to stay when that happened," Ivy said. "I don't think she's bonded with any of them since then. It's no wonder the Gideons got away with ignoring her. She encouraged them to do it."

"We're going to try and find a good foster family for her," Jack said. "Brian says he might have a few leads, and one of them is even in Shadow Lake."

"I . . . ."

Jack shifted his molten chocolate eyes down to Ivy, who was fidgeting. "You know you can't keep her, right?"

"I know," Ivy said. "I just feel that if I send her away . . . ."

"You'll be doing what that first family did to her all over again," Jack finished. "You have a huge heart, Ivy. You have a razor-sharp tongue, too, but that's a conversation for another time."

Ivy scowled as he tickled her ribs.

"You're not equipped for her," Jack said, sobering. "I know you want to help her, but in the grand scheme of things, you're the best thing for her right now. You're not the best thing for her forever."

"I know," Ivy said, resigned. "I can barely take care of myself. I've rearranged my life for her for the past few days, but that can't last forever."

"I think you're going to make a wonderful mother in the future," Jack said. "You're not ready to start that journey, though. Kelly's journey is almost over. You can't jump in at the end and fix everything."

"So, what do you suggest we do? How are we going to get Kelly to talk?"

"We're going to leave her alone tonight," Jack said. "Then, tomorrow, we're going to start asking her questions – even if she doesn't want to answer them. We have to be a united front, honey. You can't let me be the bad cop while you're the good cop and let her off the hook.

"I'm willing to let you ask the questions," he continued. "I'm willing to take a step back and let you take the lead. I need to know you're going to ask the questions without backing down, though."

"I promise," Ivy said, her voice small.

Jack reached over with his free hand and lifted her chin, searching her eyes for the truth. "I believe you can help Kelly if you start pushing her," he said. "You don't have to push hard. I think Kelly wants you to know the truth."

"Why do you think that?"

"Because it's impossible to lie to you," Jack said. "Trust me. As someone who is apparently calling you into my dreams to bear witness to the most horrible moment of my life, let me tell you something, you're not easy to shut out."

Ivy sighed. "I don't know what to do about your dreams."

"I don't either," Jack said. "We'll tackle that when we have to."

"What do we do now?"

"Now? Now I'm going to kiss you," Jack said.

Ivy's eyebrows flew up. "What? I thought we weren't dealing with this tonight?"

"We're not," Jack said. "I have to kiss you, though. I just can't seem to stop myself." Jack cut off any further argument from Ivy with his lips, pressing them to hers and sighing as she gave in and accepted the kiss. Jack pulled her tight against him, lifting her a little so he could kiss her without reservation. He was so lost in the moment, he didn't hear the approaching footsteps behind him until Max cleared his throat and Kelly started to giggle.

Jack reluctantly pulled his face away from Ivy's, although he kept his arms in place as he turned to face Max. "Has anyone ever told you that you have the worst timing ever?"

NINETEEN

"I'm sorry to interrupt your foreplay, but I was worried about Ivy," Max said, not missing a beat.

Ivy's cheeks burned under her brother's mirthful gaze. "We were just … taking a walk."

"That's what it looks like," Max said, shooting Jack a look. "Were you going to make a move on my sister out here?"

"I was not making a move on your sister," Jack argued.

Max made a face. "Really? Do you think I was born yesterday?"

"We were just … talking," Jack said.

"That's a pretty nifty trick," Max said. "Personally, I've found talking when my lips are fused to another human being practically impossible."

"You've never found talking impossible," Ivy shot back.

"Whatever," Max said, rolling his eyes. "Would you like me to take Kelly back to the house so you two can continue pawing at one another, or do you want to walk back with us?"

"We're going back," Jack said, narrowing his eyes as he regarded Max. When Ivy moved to pull away from him, he let her get far enough away so her head wasn't resting against his chest, but he snagged her hand with his and didn't let it go during the entire trek back to the cottage. Given Max's occasional glances, Jack knew the move wasn't lost on him.

Once they got back to the cottage, Kelly bounded up the steps. "I'm going to bed," she said. "I'm going to close the door in case you two want to snuggle on the couch again."

Max lifted his eyebrows. "Again?"

"They slept on the couch together last night," Kelly said.

"Thank you for tattling," Ivy said, her tone dry.

"You're welcome," Kelly said, missing the sarcasm. "I'll see you guys in the morning. Thanks for dinner, Max."

"You're very welcome, Kelly," Max said, smiling at her. Once she was gone, the smile shifted from sincere to playful. "You two are sleeping together now?"

"I … ." Ivy wasn't sure, but if it was possible for a human being's face to catch on fire, she was undergoing the phenomenon while Max teased her mercilessly and Jack did whatever he was doing as he eyed her brother.

"She was scared," Jack said. "She didn't want to wake Kelly up. There was no place else to sleep. Nothing happened."

"There's another couch in the library," Max pointed out.

Jack had forgotten about that little tidbit. "So what?"

Max held his hands up in mock surrender. "I think it's great," he said. "Personally, I would've waited until Ivy's house was empty of an impressionable teenager, but that's just me."

"I'm going to beat you," Ivy warned.

"I think Jack is going to do that for you," Max said.

"I just might," Jack said, refusing to let go of Ivy's hand even though she was trying to extricate her fingers from his. "How was Kelly tonight?"

Max reluctantly disassociated from his joyous teasing. "She was good," he said. "I showed her around town, which took all of five minutes. I took her out to Mom and Dad's and she worked in the garden with Dad for a few hours."

"She worked in the garden with Dad?" Ivy asked, surprised.

"Yeah," Max said. "Dad was careful. There were no sudden movements, and he let Kelly plant some tomatoes. Then I took her to dinner in town. Mom was making tofu, and I didn't think anyone deserved that."

"Where did you take her?" Ivy asked.

"Just to the diner."

"Did anyone ask who she was?" Jack asked.

"No," Max said, searching his memory. "People pretty much left us alone. She was fine the whole day until we got out to the parking lot."

"What happened then?" Ivy asked.

"I don't know," Max said. "I was already in my truck, and when I looked out the passenger window, I saw she was just standing there and staring at the far end of the parking lot. I said her name, but she didn't answer. She didn't even look at me.

"I got back out of the truck, but I couldn't find what she was staring at," he continued. "She finally got in the truck, and I asked her what she saw because she was kind of pale. She wouldn't tell me, though."

"You're sure you didn't see anyone?" Jack asked.

"I'm sure," Max said. "I looked hard, too. It was almost as if she'd seen a ghost. She claims she didn't see anything, but I'm not sure I believe her."

Jack rubbed the back of his neck with his free hand. "We really need her to tell us what's going on."

"I think she's close," Max said. "I know that doesn't help you two because you're not going to be able to get … carnal … while she's under the same roof, but I do think she's close."

"I'm going to kill you," Ivy seethed.

Jack ignored the exchange. "I'm going to see what I can do about tracking down the brother tomorrow," he said. "Ivy has promised to push Kelly for answers. We're stuck until Kelly decides she can't live with the secrets."

"Well, for your sake, I hope she comes clean soon," Max said.

"I hope so, too," Jack said, tugging on Ivy's hand. "Come on," he said. "I'm exhausted. I think some sleep is going to do us all some good. We can approach this fresh in the morning."

"Are you two going to sleep together on the couch again?" Max asked, his eyes twinkling.

Jack didn't answer. Instead, he offered Max a half-hearted wave as he led Ivy into the house. "Goodnight, Max."

"ARE you sure you're okay with this?" Ivy asked, her eyes flitting nervously as she regarded Jack's naked chest on the couch.

"Lay down," Jack ordered, lifting the blanket so Ivy could climb in next to him. When she was settled, he flipped the button on the lamp and plunged the room into darkness before snuggling up behind her.

"We really need to talk about what we're doing," Ivy said, her voice weary.

"Later," Jack said, resting his face against the pillow and rolling her tighter against him.

"I … I don't want to pressure you," Ivy said. "This isn't fair to you."

"Life isn't fair," Jack said. "And, in case you haven't noticed, I'm not complaining. Now shut up and go to sleep."

"Okay," Ivy said, pressing her eyes shut.

Jack's breathing was deep and regular, sleep claiming him first. Ivy wasn't far behind, and for some reason the steady beat of his heart reassured her that nothing could touch her as long as he was around.

Nothing.

"AGAIN?"

Ivy's face was incredulous when she opened her eyes and found herself on Jack's gritty dream street.

"I'm sorry," Jack said, glancing around. "I don't know why I keep doing this."

"You need me."

Jack shifted his eyes to her. "What do you mean?"

"You need me," Ivy repeated.

Jack was starting to get that. "I don't want you to see this, though," he said. "I may need you. I definitely want you. I just … don't want you to see this."

"I don't want to see it either," Ivy said, lifting her hand and pressing it to the spot above Jack's heart. "You know we're on the couch right now, right? Your arms are around me, and I can hear the beat of your heart."

"How can we be two places at once?"

Ivy shrugged. "You brought me here. You tell me."

"I don't want to keep reliving this," Jack said. "More than anything I don't want to keep dragging you into this. You should be dreaming about open fields … and picking flowers … and sandy beaches."

"So take me there," Ivy prodded.

"How?"

"Imagine where you want us to be," Ivy said. "Think hard. Don't let anything distract you." She glanced down the road, the furtive shadow closing the distance between them. "He's coming."

"I've never been in this position before in the dream," Jack said, turning quickly. "I should be on the other side of the street."

"See, you can change the dream, Jack. You're already doing it."

"I don't know how I'm doing it, though."

"Why are you here?"

"Because I dream about this almost every night." Jack was frustrated.

"No, that's not what I mean," Ivy said. "Why did you walk over here tonight."

"I … ." Jack broke off, realization dawning. "I was looking for you."

"You knew I'd be here," Ivy said. "You came for me because you wanted to protect me, even though I wasn't in danger."

"What should I do?"

"What do you want to do?" Ivy asked. "Do you want to change this dream, or move on to another dream?"

"Can I do both?"

"I'm not sure," Ivy said. "I don't understand what's going on here any more than you do. Whatever happens, though, we're going to do this together, Jack. I'm not letting you walk across that street without me."

"You're safer here."

"I'm safe there," Ivy said. "I can't die here."

"It's my dream, which means it's my subconscious," Jack argued. "The things I'm scared of in life are the same things I'm scared of in my dreams."

"I don't understand what you're trying to say."

"I'm terrified of losing you in life," Jack admitted, running his hand down the back of Ivy's head. "I can't bear the thought of it. This is my nightmare. The only thing worse than me being shot over and over again would be for you to be shot."

"Even if I'm shot in your dream, that doesn't mean I'll be hurt in real life," Ivy said, her heart rolling at Jack's words. "I'm right next to you, Jack."

"You need to run," Jack said. "He's coming for me. I won't let him hurt you."

Ivy glanced at the faceless figure. It was just a shadow. Jack wasn't allowing it to have form. He was controlling the dream without realizing it. She made up her mind quickly. "I think it's my turn to protect you," she said.

"What?"

"You keep putting yourself in danger to protect me," Ivy said. "It's my turn."

"Don't you dare," Jack warned, reaching for Ivy's hand as she moved away from him. Ivy sidestepped him neatly, shooting him a whimsical smile as she moved toward the center of the road.

"Stay there," Ivy said.

"You come back here right now," Jack said, his voice ragged.

"I'm going to be fine, Jack. I promise."

"Ivy, please." Jack was begging now, and he didn't care how pathetic he sounded. "I can't watch you be hurt. It will kill me."

"I'm not going to be hurt," Ivy said, resolute. "I'm right next to you, Jack. Your heart is beating against mine. Just remember that."

Ivy turned to face the shadow, anger coursing through her. As the shadow approached, his features evened out. Ivy didn't know what she was expecting. In her dreams, evil always looked … well … evil. This was a normal looking man, handsome even. He was shorter than Jack, although his shoulders were equally broad. His hair was dark, and his brown eyes were so dark they bordered on black.

"Who are you?" Ivy asked.

"Who are you?" the man shot back.

"I'm Ivy Morgan."

"Well, Ivy Morgan, what do you think you're doing out on the mean streets of Detroit all alone at night? A pretty little thing like you should be home. It's not safe out here."

"I'm perfectly safe," Ivy relied, nonplussed. "I'm home on my couch, a strong man wrapped around me. You're the one who doesn't belong here."

The man widened his eyes, surprised. "Are you threatening me?"

"Yes."

"Listen, little lady, I'm not the type of man you want to threaten."

The moonlight glinted off something by the man's waist, and Ivy wasn't surprised to see it was a badge. She was surprised to find the man was apparently on duty when he shot Jack. She fought the urge to turn to Jack, a million questions racing through her mind. Now wasn't the time to pressure him into an explanation.

"You don't belong here," Ivy said. "You're nothing but a figment of Jack's imagination. Sure, you existed somewhere at one time. I don't know if you do now, but you have no power here."

"I have power everywhere," the man seethed, reaching for Ivy. Before he could grab her, though, Jack was pushing between them.

"Don't touch her, Marcus."

Ivy stepped back, surprised by Jack's appearance and vehemence. He was taking control of the dream. Not because he wanted to protect himself, though. No, he was taking control of the dream to protect Ivy. Inherently, she knew he would always do just that.

"You should know better than bringing your girlfriend out here," Marcus said. "I have a job to do, and I don't care if she's a witness or not. I'll kill you both."

"You already tried to kill me, Marcus," Jack said. "You failed. I'm alive."

"I don't fail," Marcus snapped.

Jack glanced at Ivy, his eyes soft. "You're right. I can change the dream."

"Change it to something better," Ivy said.

Jack held out his hand. "Hold on."

Ivy took it, gripping it tightly, and watched as Jack shifted his gaze back to Marcus. "I don't want you coming back here," he said. "I'm not coming back here."

"Oh, really? Where are you going to go?" Marcus asked.

"Heaven," Jack replied, and as he clasped Ivy's hand so tightly she could almost swear he was cutting off the blood supply, the street tableau fell away and Ivy found herself standing in front of a river.

"Where are we?"

"This is the river by my house," Jack said.

"This is your happy place?"

"No," Jack said, shaking his head. "Although I do like the sound of the river. My happy place is here," he said, pressing his finger to the spot above Ivy's heart.

"Oh," Ivy said, her cheeks coloring.

Jack didn't give Ivy a chance to argue, or fret, or think of a reason for them both to wake up. He grabbed her, his hands snaking around the back of her head, and pressed her face against his.

This time no one interrupted their kiss, and in the real world, Ivy sighed as she snuggled closer to Jack on the couch, while he pulled her as tight as he could without smothering her.

The dream had changed, but the reality was still the same. Jack knew he wasn't going to let her go in either world. It was too late for that.

TWENTY

"Good morning, honey," Jack murmured, brushing his lips against Ivy's neck as she stirred beside him the next morning.

"Good morning," Ivy said, giving herself permission to relish his warmth for a few moments before the day beckoned.

"How did you sleep?"

"Wonderfully. How did you sleep?"

"I've never slept better," Jack said, and he was telling the truth. "I … thank you."

"I didn't do anything," Ivy said. "You changed the dream."

"I couldn't have done it if you didn't force me into a position where I had to," Jack said. "You put yourself in danger to free me."

"I was never in danger, Jack."

"Stop arguing with me," Jack said, grabbing her chin and kissing her softly.

When they parted, Ivy fixed him with a hard look. "You need to stop doing that."

"No," Jack said, pushing himself to a sitting position and running his hand through his hair.

"No?" Ivy arched a challenging eyebrow.

"No," Jack repeated.

"But … you said … ."

"I know what I said," Jack said. "I'm not saying it again, so you can stop bringing it up. I changed my mind."

"You changed your mind?" Ivy was flustered, and when she was flustered she lashed out the only way she knew how: by fighting.

"I told you last night that we're not going to talk about this until Kelly is taken care of," Jack said, turning his attention to the quiet kitchen. "Once that's finished, once it's just the two of us, then we're going to have a long talk."

"You can't make decisions for the both of us," Ivy said.

"I just did," Jack replied, unruffled. "Now, I expect you to sit there and stew for five minutes. Then I expect you to pick a fight. I'm going to cook breakfast and leave for work without engaging in said fight. By the time I get back later today, I'm hoping you'll have wrapped your head around this so we don't have to fight. If you still want to fight, though, I'll be ready then."

"You can't dictate terms in my house," Ivy said.

"Huh, and yet I'm going to do just that," Jack said, leaning over and giving her another short kiss. "And look at that, it seems to be working in my favor."

"**WHY** ARE YOU SO … GLOWY … TODAY?" Brian asked, glancing at his partner as they drove toward Gaylord. After searching through Kelly's records, Jack finally found mention of her brother. Several data scans revealed his location, and he wasn't too far away, so Jack and Brian were going to see him in person.

"I'm in a good mood," Jack said. "I slept like a rock last night."

"Did you sleep alone?" Brian was teasing, but when Jack turned to him and shook his head, he instantly sobered. "You two did it while Kelly was under the same roof?"

"We didn't do anything," Jack said. "We just slept on the couch together."

"Seriously? I thought you were anti-relationship?"

"So did I," Jack said. "It turns out, I'm full of crap when I want to be."

"So, wait, are you and Ivy officially a couple?"

"Nope," Jack replied. "We're not going to officially be anything until Kelly is safe and settled in her new home."

"Ah, that's why you're so gung-ho to find her brother, isn't it? I wondered."

"I want to find her brother because I'm hoping that he'll be willing to see Kelly," Jack said. "Something has to make her talk. I'm hoping he's going to be the one to do it."

"He hasn't seen her in eight years," Brian said. "He was in the system, too. You realize he might be just as much of a mess as she is, don't you?"

"I do," Jack said. "His record is clean, though. He's got a good job at the lumber yard out there. I'm not expecting him to come in and instantly erase all of the bad feelings Kelly has about family. I am hoping he'll be able to help, though."

"What if he doesn't want to help?"

"Then we'll figure something else out."

"When did you become a glass-half-full guy?" Brian asked, smirking. "Was it about the time you cuddled up on the couch with Ivy?"

"Maybe," Jack said. "If you're trying to rile me up about that, it isn't possible. I'm in too good of a mood."

"Because of Ivy?"

"She's part of it," Jack said. "I'm not embarrassed, so tease away."

"I have no intention of teasing you," Brian said. "Well, I probably will down the line. I don't plan on doing it now, though. I think this is great. You and Ivy have been sparking around each other since the moment you met. I have to ask, though, why now?"

"I can't fight her," Jack replied honestly. "I've tried so hard to pretend I don't have feelings for her that I've lost sight of the bigger picture."

"Which is?"

"Some things are destined," Jack said.

Brian pressed his lips together, fighting hard not to laugh. "Are you saying Ivy Morgan is your destiny?"

"I'm saying I'm done trying to live my life without Ivy in it," Jack said. "I can't do it."

"My wife is going to be so disappointed," Brian said, chuckling. "She's convinced herself she's going to find you a mate. She was crushed when I told her you were adamant about not dating."

"Your wife will survive," Jack said. "I'm not dating anyone but Ivy. Period."

"How does Ivy feel about this?" Brian asked. "She was dead set against dating, too."

"She'll come around."

"She'll come around?"

Jack sighed and pinched the bridge of his nose. "She's mad because I'm dictating terms without letting her talk about the elephant in the room," he said. "We can't talk about it until Kelly is taken care of, so she's … frustrated."

"That means she's feisty," Brian said. "You know she's going to pick a big fight, right?"

"Actually, I'm looking forward to it," Jack said, shooting his partner a cheeky grin. "Fighting with her turns me on."

"Oh boy," Brian said. "I can't wait to watch this play out."

JORDAN SISTO EYED Brian and Jack dubiously as they approached him in the lumber yard. He was tall, almost the same height as Jack, and steady hours of manual labor had turned his body into a mass of toned muscle.

"Can I help you?"

"Are you Jordan Sisto?" Jack asked, flashing his badge.

"I am. Is something wrong?"

Brian and Jack exchanged a look.

"We're here to talk to you about Kelly," Brian said, watching the man roll the idea around in his head. "Is there somewhere we can talk?"

Jordan's gaze bounced between the two men as he tried to make up his mind about what to do. Finally, he nodded and gestured for them to follow. He led them to a small clearing on the far side of the lumber yard and then turned back to them. "Is she … dead?"

"No," Jack said hurriedly. "I'm sorry. We should've led with that. I didn't mean to scare you."

Jordan exhaled heavily, relief washing over him. "I thought for sure you guys were here to tell me that she'd been killed."

"She's alive," Jack said.

"Does that mean she's been hurt?" Jordan asked.

"She has been hurt, although she's on her feet and walking around," Jack said. He explained about the past few days, watching Jordan's face as he told the story. When he was done, the younger man was hard to read. "I know that's a lot to take in."

"Can I ask when the last time you saw your sister was?" Brian asked.

"I was fifteen when my parents died," Jordan said. "I was almost sixteen actually. When I first heard about the accident, I kept trying to figure out how I was going to take care of Kelly. It never even occurred to me that we'd be separated.

"I was older than her, but I think that made it easier when my parents were still alive," he continued. "I'm sure I was jealous when they brought her home from the hospital, but I always liked her. I was her big brother, and I took my job seriously."

"That's nice," Brian said.

"When I realized the state wasn't going to let us stay in our house, I thought they would try to place us somewhere together," Jordan said. "No one wanted a teenager, though. I guess I can't blame them. I was sent to a halfway house for teenage boys until I graduated, and I thought Kelly was being adopted by a family."

"They kept her for nine months," Jack said. "Then … um … the couple got a baby and they decided they didn't want to keep Kelly."

Jordan swore under his breath. "Well, that's just great," he said. "What a stand up couple, huh? Dammit! The only reason I stayed away from her after I was released from the system was because I thought she was better off. I didn't want to disrupt her happy family life. I didn't think that was fair."

"Would you have tried to get custody of her had you known?" Brian asked.

Jordan faltered. "I don't know," he admitted. "I was eighteen, and I doubt the state would've given her to me. I can't say if I would've tried or not, though. I just ... I don't know. I know I wouldn't have been a good guardian then. It took me some time to get on my feet.

"I found a good job, though," he said. "I'm happy here. I'm never going to be rich, but the owner took a chance on me. Now I go to his house every Sunday for family dinner. I'm working my way up through the ranks here. He's teaching me about the business end. He says ... he says he wants to sell the business to me when he's ready to retire."

"That's amazing," Jack said. "You've done well for yourself. Most kids in your situation would've had trouble surviving, let alone thriving. You should proud of yourself. I'm sure your parents would be."

"Would they?" Jordan asked, his face serious. "I can't help but think they'd be disappointed because of what I let happen to Kelly."

"You can't think that way, son," Brian said. "You had no way of knowing."

"What happened to her?" Jordan asked.

"We don't know yet," Jack said. "She's not talking about it, and that's actually why we came looking for you."

"You want me to talk to her, don't you?"

"Do you think you're up for that?" Brian asked.

"She's my sister," Jordan said. "I'm willing to do what it takes to make sure she's okay."

"You're a good kid," Jack said. "Man, I mean. You're a good man."

"Don't worry about it," Jordan said. "I still feel like a kid. When do you want me to talk to her?"

Jack and Brian exchanged a look.

"Can you come over to Shadow Lake tonight?" Jack asked. "I'd like you to have dinner with Kelly. I'll be there, too, as will the woman Kelly is staying with. We can make sure to give you some time alone.

If that goes well, I'd like you two to spend some more time together, too."

"What if she doesn't want to see me?" Jordan asked.

"Kelly is desperate for family," Jack said. "I don't know a lot, but I do know that. She might be difficult at first. I'm not going to lie. She's got a lot of resentment built up."

"I guess she's earned that," Jordan said. "I'll talk to my boss. When I explain what's going on, he'll give me whatever time I need off. Give me directions."

Jack clapped him on the shoulder. "Thank you."

"You're going out of your way to protect my sister," Jordan said. "I'm the one who should be thanking you."

TWENTY-ONE

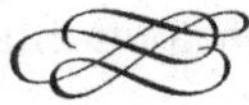

"I don't know about this," Kelly said, eyeing the horse suspiciously as Ivy showed her how to get in the saddle. "What if it bites me?"

"Horses don't bite."

"I … do you know all horses?" Kelly narrowed her eyes, and Ivy had to suck her cheeks in to keep from laughing out loud.

"These are gentle horses," Ivy said. "I've ridden them hundreds of times. They know the paths. They can't get lost. They won't break into a run without prodding – and I'm guessing you're not going to prod this one."

"Can't we just go for a walk?" Kelly pleaded.

Ivy tilted her head to the side, considering. "We can go for a walk instead if you tell me what's going on."

Kelly made a face. "You're blackmailing me?"

"I like to consider it aggressive negotiations," Ivy countered.

"I don't want to talk about it."

"Then get on the horse."

"But … ."

Ivy shook her head, the look on her face no-nonsense and firm. "Get on the horse, Kelly."

Once the teenager was settled with the reins in her hands, Ivy climbed up on her own horse and led the way out of the barn. The horses in question knew the paths to take, and Ivy let her steed lead the way as Kelly's kept pace next to her.

"See, it's not trying to bite you," Ivy said.

"It could be thinking about it."

Ivy chuckled despite herself. "Is this your first time on a horse?"

"The Gideons weren't big on spending money on things that didn't benefit them," Kelly said, not bothering to hide the bitterness in her voice.

"I'm sorry you had to live with them," Ivy said. "I … there are no words for how sorry I am."

"It's not your fault," Kelly said. "You don't have to apologize."

"You're never going to have to see them again," Ivy said. "Don't worry about it. In fact, Brian left me a message. He had someone drive over to the house and pick all your stuff up. He's going to send it with Jack tonight."

"Jack is spending the night again?" Kelly asked, lifting her eyebrows suggestively. "Did you two do it last night?"

"You're obsessed with us *doing it*," Ivy said, making a face. "I think you need to let it go."

"I'm taking that as a no."

"What makes you say that?"

"Because you would be in a better mood if it was a yes," Kelly teased.

Ivy couldn't help herself from smirking. "Jack and I are … in limbo right now."

Kelly sobered. "Because of me?"

"Because of a lot of things," Ivy said. "I don't want you to worry about that. Jack and I have issues of our own. We have a few things to talk about."

"I don't think Jack wants to talk," Kelly said. "I think Jack wants to kiss you."

"Jack has very busy lips," Ivy said. "He wants to flap them just as much as he wants to use them for kissing."

"Whatever," Kelly said, rolling her eyes. "I saw you two at the fairy ring last night. It didn't look like talking was on his mind."

"Let's talk about something else," Ivy suggested.

"Like what?" Kelly asked.

"Do you know what Jack is doing today?"

"Daydreaming about kissing you?"

Ivy made a face. "No more talking about that," she ordered. "I don't want to even think about Jack's lips for the rest of the day."

"You're the one who brought up Jack," Kelly reminded her.

"That's because he's on a special errand today," Ivy said.

"Oh, yeah? What errand? Is he riding a horse, too?"

"He's in Gaylord," Ivy said. "He found your brother."

Kelly's shoulders stiffened, and her eyes were full of trepidation when she shifted them to Ivy. "He did? He found Jordan?"

"I don't know a lot yet," Ivy cautioned. "I do know Jordan has done well for himself. He works at the lumber yard out there, and he wants to see you."

"I don't want to see him."

"He's coming for dinner tonight," Ivy said, Jack's words about not backing down playing through the back of her mind. "You're going to be civil."

"He abandoned me."

"He was sixteen years old," Ivy argued. "He didn't abandon you. Jack didn't have a lot of time to talk on the phone, but he did tell me that Jordan tried to keep you, but the state wouldn't let him."

"He could've kept me if he wanted to." Kelly wasn't giving up on the scenario she'd built in her mind over the past eight years.

"The state wouldn't allow that," Ivy said.

"What about after he was eighteen?"

"Jordan thought you were adopted," Ivy said, choosing her words carefully. "He thought the couple you first went to live with kept you this whole time. Now, I know that's a sore subject, and I don't want to make it worse, but he thought he was doing the right thing."

"How does forgetting I existed equate to 'the best thing'?" Kelly challenged.

"He thought he would be doing more harm than good by interrupting your life," Ivy said. "Jack said he was really upset when he found out the truth."

"He was?" Despite her belligerence, Ivy couldn't help but notice the touch of hope in Kelly's voice.

"He's coming to see you tonight, isn't he?"

"Jack probably made him," Kelly grumbled.

"Jack wouldn't do something like that," Ivy said. "You need to give Jack a break."

"Because you're kissing him?"

"Because he's trying to help you," Ivy shot back. "Now … ride your horse. If you don't stop talking about Jack and kissing, I'm going to tell that horse to bite you."

"You don't have the power," Kelly scoffed.

"**MAKE** SURE YOU BRUSH HIM DOWN," Ivy instructed, glancing over Kelly's shoulder as she watched the teenager work.

"I don't understand why we have to do this," Kelly complained. "Isn't that what the stable hands are for?"

"You're going to bond with that horse or spend the night here," Ivy said.

"Whatever," Kelly said, rolling her eyes.

Ivy shuffled across the barn, not stopping until she was next to Millie Nixon. "I forgot how obnoxious teenagers were."

Millie, who also happened to be Brian's wife, snorted. "I remember some particularly obnoxious days with Sean and Simon when they were that age," she said, referring to her sons. "Sometimes you and Max joined in and made it a free-for-all."

"How many days are you working here now?"

"Just once a week," Millie said. "I volunteer my time because I love the horses. Brian says we're too busy to have any out at the farm, and I agree with him, but I miss having them around."

"I kind of wish you guys still had horses, too," Ivy said. "I would've brought her out there instead of here if I had the chance."

Millie lowered her voice. "Are you worried about someone seeing her? Brian says someone broke into your house the other night."

Ivy shrugged. "Whoever wants her knows where she's staying," she said. "I'm more concerned with answering hard questions from well-meaning people. How do I explain who she is?"

"Just leave that to me if it comes up," Millie said.

"Why you?"

"I'm a better liar than you are."

Ivy snorted. "I'll have you know, I'm a world-class liar when I want to be."

"Sweetie, you're the worst liar ever," Millie said. "Every time you tried to lie when you were a teenager the tops of your ears turned red. That's how I always caught you and Max when you were up to no good."

"And then you called and told our parents," Ivy reminded her.

"That's what friends do in a town this small," Millie replied, nonplussed. "Speaking of Max, when do you think he's going to settle down?"

"Not any time soon," Ivy said. "Aunt Felicity called him a hound dog yesterday, and I'm starting to think that should be his new nickname. Spread the word."

Millie chuckled. "Your brother has a mile-long streak of charm, that's for sure," she said. "Still, I think someone is going to tame him one day, and when they do, he's going to make a fine husband and father. Don't worry about it. He still has plenty of time."

"I'm not worried about it," Ivy said. "I think my mother would like a few grandkids, though."

"Maybe you and Jack will give her some."

Ivy turned swiftly, fixing Millie with a hard look as the woman pretended to study Kelly and the horse. "What did you just say?"

"I said that your hair is very pretty," Millie lied.

"No, what did you say about Jack? Who told you that?"

Millie sighed. "Sweetie, let it go. Everyone in this town knows about you and Jack. All the single female hearts are breaking, and all the male egos are taking a pounding."

"What has Brian told you?" Ivy asked, narrowing her eyes.

"Brian told me to mind my own business," Millie said. "I've had my eye on Jack for some random fix-ups ever since I heard he was coming to town. Brian said the minute you two laid eyes on each other fireworks started going off, though, so I decided to take a step back and hedge my bets."

"I don't know what that means."

"I've always wanted you to find someone to tame that wild streak," Millie said. "You weren't ready, though. I didn't even consider you for Jack when I heard he was coming to town because I didn't think you would be ready for a long while. It looks like I was wrong on that front."

"Jack and I are … not together."

"Oh, please," Millie said, waving off Ivy's argument. "You and Jack can keep telling people you're not together, but everyone knows it's only a matter of time. People saw you playing basketball at the high school together."

"How does that equate to being a couple?"

"People know he's been staying out at your house the past two nights."

"On the couch," Ivy said, refusing to own up to the fact that she'd been on the couch with him. "He's staying to make sure Kelly is safe."

"Keep telling yourself that," Millie said. "You're going to have to find another excuse when Kelly is gone, though."

"I … ." Ivy broke off, frustrated. "Everyone in this town thinks this is so funny. It's not going to be funny when Jack breaks my heart."

Millie shifted her eyes to Ivy. "What do you mean?"

"He doesn't want a relationship," Ivy said. "Even if I did want one … which I don't, mind you … he doesn't want to be tied down."

Millie pursed her lips. "Everyone says that until they find the one they're supposed to be with," she said. "You're tying yourself up in knots because you're terrified he is the one for you. Don't make yourself sick over this. Things will work out how they're supposed to."

"And you think they're going to work out in a way that lets Jack and I be together?"

"I don't think that," Millie said, and despite herself, Ivy's heart sank at the words. "I *know* you're going to be together."

Ivy faltered. "How?"

"Some things are destiny," Millie said. "I have faith you and Jack are destiny."

"I wish I had your faith," Ivy said.

"Don't worry. You will."

"I . . . ."

"Who is that?" Millie asked, cutting Ivy off and pointing toward the far end of the barn. "That guy has been standing there for ten minutes, and he's been staring at Kelly the whole time. I don't recognize him."

Ivy swiveled, fixing her eyes on the dark figure in question. The barn wasn't well lit, and even though the sun was still relatively high in the sky, she couldn't make out his features. All she could see was that he looked to be of average height and weight, and Millie was right, he was focused on Kelly.

"I don't know," Ivy said. "Watch Kelly."

"What are you going to do?" Millie asked.

"Find out who he is," Ivy said. "I'd like to do it without freaking Kelly out if I can."

"You be careful," Millie warned. "Don't do anything stupid."

"I never do stupid things," Ivy said, striding off in the direction of the stranger. She kept her pace even, but purposeful, and after a few moments, the stranger shifted his eyes from Kelly to Ivy. Ivy still couldn't make out his features, but whatever the man was hoping to accomplish was cut short when he turned on his heel and walked out of the barn.

Ivy broke into a run. "Hey!"

By the time she raced out of the barn, the area surrounding it was empty. She scanned the open expanse, hoping to see a glimpse of the man. When she heard a car engine fire up, she shifted her attention to the parking lot just in time to see a red Ford Explorer speed out. She was too far away to get the license plate.

"Crap," she muttered, reaching for her phone. "Jack is not going to like this."

TWENTY-TWO

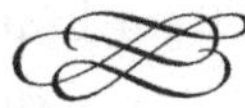

"So, let me get this straight . . . ." Jack pinched the bridge of his nose to keep from shaking Ivy, frustration bubbling up as he internally warned himself that picking a fight – especially now, when Jordan was on his way – would be a bad idea. "After your house was broken into and you were thrown into a wall, you took it upon yourself to chase a stranger. Is that what you're telling me?"

"Don't you even think of yelling at me," Ivy warned, her eyes narrowing. "I didn't realize I was going to be chasing him. I just wanted to know why he was staring at Kelly. It was broad daylight, and there were people around."

"I'm going to have to . . . ." Jack broke off, miming strangling her.

Ivy had to purse her lips to keep from smiling. He was cute when he was animated. "Is that some form of interpretive dance? I didn't know you were into that."

"Don't push me," Jack said, extending a finger in Ivy's direction. "I will spank your bottom blue."

Ivy scowled. "And yet you say that like it's going to turn you on."

"Oh, you have no idea, honey," Jack said. He placed his hands on his hips and looked over Ivy's shoulder so he could watch Kelly on the swing in the front yard. While she'd displayed reticence to the announcement that her brother was on his way, she was keenly nervous while waiting for him.

Ivy followed his gaze, nervous butterflies flitting through her own stomach. "You're sure he wants to see her, right? She can't take another disappointment."

"I'm sure," Jack said. "He feels guilty. He honestly thought he was doing the right thing."

"It sounds like he's done well for himself," Ivy said. "Maybe they'll be able to work something out so they can see each other on a regular basis. When Kelly is released from the system, she'll have someone on the outside to help her."

"He's done amazingly well for himself," Jack said. "He's soft-spoken, he's kind, and he's a hard worker."

"Good," Ivy said. "I suppose I should get inside and make dinner."

"I brought steaks," Jack said, reaching for the bag he'd dropped on the lawn chair when he approached Ivy upon his return to her house.

Ivy made a face. "I don't like steak."

"I didn't buy one for you," Jack said. "I figured you can eat your … asparagus burger … while the rest of us eat real food. I'm sure you can handle the sides."

"You're really pushing your luck," Ivy said, grabbing the bag from him and glancing inside. "I don't even know how to cook these."

"I guess it's good you have a world-class griller here to help you then," Jack said, grabbing the bag back from her. "Don't touch those. You'll get … alfalfa sprouts cooties all over them."

"I'm going to give you cooties," Ivy threatened.

"That's what I'm hoping for," Jack said, swatting her rear to prod her into the house. "We have to get Kelly taken care of first, though."

"Stop saying things like that."

Jack waited until they were safely inside the house – and away from Kelly's prying eyes – before grabbing the front of her shirt and pushing her against the wall. "No." His eyes were soulful as he dropped a soft kiss on her mouth.

Despite the warning in the back of her mind telling her to pull away, Ivy returned the hot kiss. When Jack finally pulled away, Ivy had to check herself briefly to make sure she was still dressed, and then she fixed him with an icy stare. "You're really full of yourself."

Jack smiled, loving the pouty look on her face. "I can't wait until we have some time alone together. I'm going to show you just how full of myself I am."

Secretly, Ivy was looking forward to that, too.

JORDAN WAS nervous as he hopped out of his truck in Ivy's driveway. Jack met him on the front porch, a welcoming smile in place as the younger man trudged up the steps.

"Did you have trouble finding the place?" Jack asked.

"Your directions were good," Jordan said. "I didn't see the house at first because of the trees, but I realized where it was once I passed by. I didn't overshoot it by much."

"That's good."

"This is a cool place," Jordan said, scanning the property. "Do you live here?"

"I live over on the river," Jack said. "The land is great. The house is a dump."

"And this house belongs to … what did you say her name was?"

"Ivy Morgan," Jack said. "If she runs hot and cold on you, don't worry about it. I'm the one irritating her right now."

"How did you do that?"

Jack tilted his head to the side, considering. "I won't stop kissing her."

Jordan snorted. "I see."

"It's a long story," Jack said.

"I'm guessing it's one of those stories that's going to have a happy ending," Jordan said.

"I'm starting to think that myself," Jack said. "Don't worry, she's a wonderful woman. She just has attitude."

"All the best ones do," Jordan said, sucking in a deep breath. "I'm ready."

"It's going to be okay," Jack said, patting him on the shoulder.

"Kelly has been looking forward to seeing you all day, even if she won't admit it. Just ... be prepared for her to be hostile for the first few minutes. She's got a lot of resentment pent up about what's happened to her throughout the years."

"I don't blame her," Jordan said. "When do you want me to start questioning her about what happened?"

"Don't force it," Jack said. "Get to know her first. We've survived this long. Another couple of hours isn't going to kill us." At least Jack hoped that was the truth. He led Jordan into the small cottage and pointed toward the patio through the back sliding glass door. "She's out there."

Jordan stared for a moment, his heart clenching when he saw Kelly. He would've recognized her anywhere. Even though eight years had passed – eight important ones for Kelly – it was almost as if he was staring at a younger version of their mother when he saw her animatedly talking to the woman next to the grill.

"Ivy has pink hair," Jordan said.

"Some of it is pink," Jack replied. "I thought it was weird at first, too. It fits her personality, though."

"Her personality is pink?" Jordan arched an eyebrow.

"Her personality is fiery," Jack said. "Come on. I'll introduce you. Besides, I don't trust her with those steaks alone."

Jack pushed open the door, ushering Jordan out in front of him. Kelly's gaze locked with her brother's the second she saw him, and Ivy couldn't help but notice Jordan clasped his hands together – the same way Kelly did when she was nervous – when he saw his sister for the first time in eight years.

"Hey, trouble."

Kelly opened her mouth to respond, years of anger and bitterness ready to pour out like a waterfall. Instead, she burst into tears and rushed to him, letting him hug her as he shed a few tears of his own.

Jack moved away, offering them some privacy, and edged Ivy away from the grill with his hips as he took the pronged fork from her and flipped the steaks wordlessly. Ivy watched the brother and sister cry, her heart flopping, and then lifted her glassy eyes to Jack's. He bent over and kissed her on the nose quickly before shifting his attention back to the grill. "I see you didn't burn them."

"I … ." Ivy wrinkled her nose. "I'm perfectly capable of cooking cow flesh."

"I love it when you refer to it that way," Jack said. "It gives me this low-down tickle in my stomach."

"I'm going to tickle you." Ivy realized what she'd said and made a face. "Wait. That came out wrong."

"Oh, no," Jack teased. "I think it came out exactly right."

"You're a pig," Ivy said.

"Oink."

"THIS LOOKS GREAT," Jordan said, smiling appreciatively as Ivy slipped a heaping plate of steak, potatoes, mushrooms and vegetables in front of him. "I can't remember the last time I had a home-cooked meal like this."

"Me either," Kelly said, her eyes widening at her own plate. "Wow. This is even better than Jack's breakfasts."

"Jack cooks you breakfast?" Jordan asked, intrigued.

"He's been sleeping on the couch," Kelly said. "Ivy has been sleeping with him, but I'm not supposed to talk about it. She told me today that she was going to gag me if I didn't stop talking about Jack kissing her."

Ivy scorched Kelly with a look while Jack smirked. "Don't worry. I won't let her gag you. Keep bugging her about the kisses. I like it when she gets flustered."

"You like it when she does anything," Kelly countered. "Max says you're hot for her bod."

Jack faltered. "I'm going to gag Max, that's for sure."

"Who is Max?" Jordan asked, reaching for the steak sauce.

"He's my brother," Ivy explained. "He's been out here a few times helping with some stuff, and he took Kelly to dinner last night."

"He's really hot," Kelly said, her giggle belying her age as her eyes looked years beyond it.

"Don't say things like that," Ivy said. "Max has a big enough ego as it is."

"Max says he's God's gift to women," Kelly said. "He told me he thought Jack was going to be his competition until Jack saw you. Then he knew he was safe."

"Yup, I'm definitely gagging Max," Jack said.

"What are you doing to me?" Max picked that moment to appear from the side of the house. He climbed the patio, grabbing a chair and pushing it between Ivy and Kelly. Once he settled, his gaze fell on Jordan. "Who are you?"

"I'm Kelly's brother, Jordan. You must be the infamous Max I've heard so much about."

"I am," Max said, extending his hand in greeting. "Don't worry if your sister has a crush on me. No woman is immune."

Jordan smirked, Max's charm winning him over almost instantaneously. Ivy cuffed the back of Max's head. "Who invited you to dinner?" she asked.

"I invited myself," Max replied, nonplussed. "I brought the paint you wanted for your front door. I figured you would want to reward me with a good meal. I can't believe you made steak."

"Jack made steak," Ivy corrected.

"Good, then Jack is going to give me half of his," Max said.

"You can have half of mine," Kelly offered.

"Oh, no," Max said, winking. "Jack is dating my sister. He owes me."

"I don't owe you anything," Jack shot back, but he was already sawing his steak in half. He speared the smaller portion with his fork and dropped it on Max's plate. "I just happen to think rewarding you for fixing your sister's door is worth a piece of meat. If you'd told me you were coming, I would've bought you your own."

"You should sign up for my newsletter," Max said, his eyes sparkling. "Then you would always know where I am, just like my rabid female fans."

"You have a newsletter?" Kelly asked, her eyes widening.

"Don't listen to a word he says," Ivy chided. "He's full of it."

"Listen, little sister, I'm the one who put a new door on your house after it got kicked in," Max said. "I'm the one who agreed to paint it because you didn't like the color. I'm the one who … I want some mushrooms."

Ivy sighed and tipped half of her mushrooms onto his plate.

"Where was I?" Max asked.

"Right about to the point where I was looking for something to gag you with," Jack said.

"Wait, your door got kicked in?" Jordan asked, interrupting the friendly family banter. "How did that happen?"

Ivy and Jack exchanged a look. Now was the time.

"I think that's something you need to ask Kelly," Jack said carefully.

Jordan shifted his attention to his sister. "Is there something you want to tell me?"

Kelly swallowed hard, unsure. "I … ."

"Let's eat dinner first," Ivy said, swooping in quickly. "We'll talk about all of this when the food isn't getting cold."

"Ivy," Jack warned.

"It can wait a half hour, Jack. Let everyone enjoy their meal."

"Fine," Jack grumbled, turning back to his plate.

"You're so whipped already," Max cackled.

"I'm seriously going to gag you, Max," Jack said, although the smile he sent Ivy was warm. "You and I are going to have our own little talk after dinner, Mr. Morgan."

TWENTY-THREE

"Thank you for dinner," Jordan said, handing Ivy his plate as she rinsed dishes and slipped them in the dishwasher. "I really appreciate it."

"I really appreciate you coming here," Ivy said, her eyes serious. "Kelly needs you in your life."

Jordan stilled. "I . . . ."

"I'm not asking you to take everything on yourself," Ivy said quickly. "I know you're young, and the things you've gone through are just as bad as the things Kelly's gone through. I'm just hoping you'll be able to visit her from time to time."

"I won't lose her again," Jordan promised. "You know, you taking her in is a miracle. Most people in your position would've called the cops and sent her on her way."

"I'm not most people."

"No, you're not," Jordan agreed, shifting his head so he could watch Jack, Max, and Kelly cavorting outside. "Your brother is good with her, too."

"Max is good with everyone," Ivy said. "Don't get me wrong, he's a rampant pain in the rear end, but he's got a heart of gold."

"And what about Jack?"

"He's been wonderful with her."

"That's not what I meant," Jordan said, teasing. "Does he have a heart of gold, too? Don't bother denying it. I see the way you two look at each other. It can't be easy on you."

"Jack is a good man," Ivy said, choosing her words carefully. "We are not in a relationship, though."

"Yet," Jordan said. "Something tells me the thing holding you back right now is Kelly. That doesn't seem fair to the two of you."

"We're adults," Ivy said. "We have a few things to … discuss … before anything happens. We're going to make sure Kelly is settled and safe. I promise you that."

"You need her to talk to do that," Jordan said. "That's one of the reasons I'm here."

"I want you to bond with your sister," Ivy said. "I know Jack prodded you into coming so you could talk with her, but you don't have to force that issue tonight."

"Jack wants you to be safe," Jordan said. "I understand that. As long as Kelly is hiding something, neither one of you is safe. I want Kelly safe just as much as Jack wants you safe."

"Just … be careful," Ivy said. "She gets upset when you push her. She's starting to volunteer more and more information, but whatever secret she's keeping has to be a doozy – at least from her limited viewpoint."

"What do you mean?" Jordan asked, genuinely curious.

"Don't you remember what it was like to be sixteen? Everything is magnified when you're that age. All the heartbreaks are bigger, and all the embarrassments seem like they're things you're never going to get over."

"Someone is trying to grab her," Jordan said. "Someone is willing to kill you to get her. That doesn't seem like an exaggeration to me."

"That's not what I meant," Ivy said. "I don't disagree that she knows something important. I think she's convinced herself that her reasons for keeping it secret are somehow dire. That's what I was getting at."

"Oh," Jordan said, tapping his chin thoughtfully. "You think she's convinced herself that whatever perceived embarrassment comes from telling the truth is going to be worse than someone trying to hurt her … and you."

"Exactly," Ivy said.

"Well, we can't let her think that," Jordan said. "Do you have any suggestions on getting her to talk?"

"Actually, I do," Ivy said, her face sober as she regarded Jordan. "Just how far are you willing to go to keep your sister safe?"

"As far as it takes," Jordan said truthfully. "What do you want me to do?"

"**JORDAN** AND IVY are sure taking a long time doing dishes in there," Kelly said, glancing up toward the house as she chewed on her lower lip. "Do you think I should see what they're doing?"

"They're finishing the dishes," Max said. "They'll be out in a second. Don't worry about it."

"Max is right," Jack said. "Ivy and Jordan will be out in a second."

"Max is always right," Kelly said, giggling.

Max winked at her. "See, a woman after my own heart. She knows quality when she sees it."

"She's too young to see all the smoke you're blowing out of your … ." Jack broke off when he heard the front door opening. Ivy and Jordan filed out. Both of them were smiling, but Jack could detect a small shift in the way they were carrying themselves. "Here they come."

Kelly turned, smiling when she saw Jordan walking in her direction. "I thought you two got lost in there."

"We were just having a discussion," Jordan said.

"What about?"

"You."

Kelly faltered. "I … you want to know what happened to me, don't you?"

"Yes," Jordan said.

"I don't want to talk about it." Kelly jutted her lower lip out.

"That's not going to work on me," Jordan said. "You forget, I'm your big brother. I remember when you used to do that to get your own way when you were a kid. We need to have a talk, kid. It's time you tell us what's really going on."

"I don't want to talk about it!"

"You have to," Jordan said, refusing to back down. "Mom and Dad raised us to tell the truth, Kelly. I know you don't remember them as well as I do, but they would be disappointed to think you were lying."

"Don't say that," Kelly hissed.

"Just tell us what's going on."

"Kelly, I know you think that keeping whatever this is a secret is the way to go," Ivy said. "I promise you, whatever it is, we're going to help you. We're going to find a way to make this right. We can't do that if we don't know what's going on."

"I … ." Kelly's eyes darted from face to face, conflicted.

"Do you know what I remember most about you when you were a kid?" Jordan asked, changing tactics. "I remember you used to race home from school because you knew Mom was waiting for you. She always had a pot of tea ready in the winter, and you two would sit at the counter and gossip.

"You'd tell her about all the things you did during the day," he continued. "You'd tell her about how a boy smiled at you, or how one of your friends made fun of you, or even how you were going to marry that one boy – I can't remember his name – who tied his jacket around his neck in the middle of winter and pretended he was Superman."

"Jackson Douglas," Kelly said, making a face. "I can't believe you remember that."

"I remember it all, Kelly," Jordan said. "I remember that I got home later from school because I had basketball practice. I remember that we would all eat dinner together as a family. Dad would tell us about his day at the resort. Do you remember that?"

"What resort?" Max asked.

"Shanty Creek," Jordan replied. "Do you remember that, Kelly? He worked in security. It wasn't dangerous or anything. His biggest hassle was usually dealing with underage drinkers and the occasional loudmouth who raised a ruckus at the bar."

"I kind of remember that," Kelly hedged. "I … I remember he took us up there in the winter so we could see the tree lighting ceremony. It was the biggest tree ever. He would buy us hot chocolate, and then we'd go and sit on Santa's lap and tell him what we wanted for Christmas."

"You did that," Jordan said, shooting a look in Max's direction. "I was not sitting on Santa's lap when I was fifteen."

"I'm sure you weren't," Max said.

"I'm just making sure you know that because you seem like the type of guy who gets off on teasing people," Jordan said. "I don't want you going off on a tangent because you think I was sitting on Santa's lap as a teenager."

Ivy snickered. "Don't worry about it. Max believed in Santa until he was thirteen."

"I did not," Max scoffed.

"You did so," Ivy said. "You were crushed when Dad finally sat you down and told you. I got grounded when I told you, and I was younger than you."

"Shut up," Max said, wagging a finger in Ivy's face.

"You believed in Santa when you were thirteen?" Kelly asked, entertainment flitting across her features. "Wow."

"I'll have you know, I still believe in Santa," Max replied, guileless. "I don't care who tells me otherwise. I'm always going to believe."

"It's okay to believe in whatever you want to believe in, Kelly," Ivy said. "No one wants to take away your belief system. I am worried that you're keeping this secret for the wrong reasons, though."

"Whatever it is, we're going to stand with you," Jack said. "You have to tell us the truth. That's the only way we can move forward."

"I … can't," Kelly said. "It's too horrible."

Jack pushed the heel of his hand against his forehead, frustrated. "Kelly, whoever is after you is willing to hurt anyone who gets in his way," he said. "Whoever this man is, he kicked down Ivy's door. He threw her into a wall. She was willing to die to protect you. I don't want that. I don't think you do either."

"Of course I don't," Kelly said, her voice cracking. "It's just … you'll hate me."

"We could never hate you," Ivy said. "We've all made mistakes. Every single person here has made mistakes. That's how you grow as a person. No one can go through life without making mistakes. It's impossible."

"She's right," Max said. "She should know, she made a mountain of them when she was your age."

"She did?" Kelly asked hopefully.

"She did," Max said. "She dated a guy who cheated on her with everyone in town. As an adult, he bought liquor for kids just so he could have someone to hang around with. Then he started his own cult."

"I'm so glad you're focusing on me," Ivy grumbled.

Jack rubbed the back of her neck soothingly. "Let's focus on me," he said, drawing Kelly's attention away from Ivy. "You know Ivy and I were fighting the other day, don't you? Do you know why?"

"Because she invaded your privacy," Kelly said.

"That's … kind of why," Jack said. "She didn't really invade my privacy. I was upset and lashed out at her because that's how I saw it at the time, but the truth is, I was having trouble dealing with a secret of my own."

"Does it have to do with those scars on your chest?" Kelly asked.

Jack swallowed hard. "I … ."

"Kelly, it's not important what Jack's secret is," Ivy started, working overtime to try and help Jack out of a sticky situation.

"Yes, it is," Jack said, interrupting her. "We can't ask Kelly to tell her secret if I'm keeping one, can we?"

"Jack … ."

Jack ignored her. "I didn't always work as a police officer in Shadow Lake," he said. "I used to work in Detroit. While I was down there, I found out my partner was doing some illegal things. Instead of turning him in right away, I confronted him and told him that he had to turn himself in.

"That was a mistake," he continued. "I … I did the wrong thing. I thought I was doing it for the right reasons, but I wasn't. It backfired on me. Instead of turning himself in, my partner hunted me down on the streets like a dog and he … shot me … twice."

Max's mouth dropped open. "Holy crap."

Jordan's eyes widened at Jack's admission. "Wow."

Ivy put her hand on Jack's waist to anchor him. She was the only one who could know exactly what he'd just given up, and she'd never been prouder of anyone in her entire life. All of the reasons for not dating him flew out the window at that moment, and all she could think about was kissing him again. Sadly, they had an audience.

"Did you almost die?" Kelly asked.

"Yes," Jack replied. "I was in a coma for three days, and I was in the hospital for three weeks. I made a mistake, and I almost paid the ultimate price. I don't want the same thing to happen to you."

"I … ." Kelly's gaze bounced from serious face to serious face. "Can I think about it tonight? Can I please have tonight?"

"I … ." Ivy wanted to tell her yes, but she didn't know if it was the right thing to do.

"You can have tonight," Jack said carefully. "Tomorrow you have to start talking, though. I want you to think long and hard about what happened, and I want you to get yourself together however you have to so you can tell us what we need to know."

Kelly nodded solemnly and took a step forward. Ivy was surprised when the teenager gave Jack a hug. It was small and tentative, but Jack returned it. When Kelly stepped back, her face was a myriad of unexpressed emotions. "I'm going to go to bed now. I … just need to think."

"Okay," Ivy said.

"I'll walk you back to the house and say goodbye," Jordan said. "We'll make plans to get together again."

"Really?" Kelly asked, her eyebrows lifting.

"You're not shaking me again, kid," Jordan said. "We're going to figure out a way so I can have regular visitation. It's all going to work out. I promise."

Max, Jack, and Ivy watched brother and sister shuffle toward the house. Once they were inside, Max turned his attention to Jack and Ivy. "I'm going to put off the painting for a few days," he said. "You can live with the ugly color for now, Ivy. I … you're the bravest man I know, Jack. I'm proud you're dating my sister."

"We're not dating," Ivy said.

Max snorted. "Shut up and give the poor guy a break. I think, after tonight, he deserves it." He started moving toward his truck. "Oh, and Jack? Your secret is safe with me."

Ivy watched her brother go, love bubbling up. Once he was out of the driveway, she kept her eyes from Jack's face – frightened to see the emotion percolating there – and wrapped her arms around his waist as she hugged him. "You're the bravest man I know, too."

Jack pulled her tight, dropping a kiss on the top of her head. "Let's hope it's enough," he said. "We can't wait another day for her to tell us the truth. I have this feeling … we're running out of time."

Ivy had the same feeling.

TWENTY-FOUR

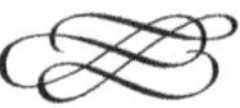

"Good morning, honey," Jack said, kissing Ivy's neck as he pulled her close the next morning. This was starting to feel like his morning routine, and he was enjoying it. He couldn't help but think he would enjoy it more if they were in a bed, but for now, he didn't have the energy to complain.

"Good morning," Ivy murmured.

"How did you sleep?"

"Good," Ivy said. "I really enjoyed your dream about taking me fishing, by the way. That was a special kind of torture."

Jack smirked. He loved fishing. When he'd directed his dream in that direction, he'd forgotten to take Ivy's vegetarianism into account. Still, the arguing was a turn on – like it always was. "No one said you had to fish. You could've watched me fish."

"You challenged me to a fishing competition," Ivy said. "I couldn't ignore that – especially when I knew that we weren't killing real fish."

"I still won."

"I let you win," Ivy countered. "I didn't think your manhood could take being beaten by a girl."

"My manhood is not up for debate," Jack said, grinding himself against her softly to let her know what he was referring to.

"Oh," Ivy said, her eyes widening. "I . . . ."

"It's not time to talk about it yet," Jack cautioned.

"But . . . it's kind of right there."

"It is," Jack agreed. "It's the morning. That can't be held against me."

"Apparently it can be held against me, though," Ivy said. Despite her words, she didn't pull away from him. "Do you think I can pick dream activities in the future? I don't mean every night, but if we're going to be sharing dreams, I'd like to be in charge occasionally."

"Oh, honey, you're going to be in charge whenever you want," Jack said, kissing her neck again. "I . . . ugh . . . we need to get this Kelly situation taken care of. I'm not sure how much more of this I can take."

"What happens if you change your mind once Kelly is gone?" Ivy asked, her voice small. "I . . . what if you're only feeling this because you've been around me so much lately."

She was worried. Jack knew why, and he didn't blame her. "Honey, I've been feeling this since I met you. I . . . I really don't want to have this conversation when we could be interrupted. Please, just have faith in me. We'll talk about this when it's just the two of us."

"Okay," Ivy said, giving in.

"I do have one question," Jack said, glancing down to the spot at the end of the couch where their feet were tangled together. "Why do you always poke your feet out from the end of the blanket? You've done it every night we've been together. I've woken up in the middle of the night and covered your feet, and yet every morning when I wake up, they're poking out from under the covers again."

"I don't know," Ivy mused. "I've just always done it. Even when it's the middle of the winter I like my feet out from under the covers. I can't explain it."

"I find it cute," Jack said. "I have no idea why, though."

"Your feet are out, too," Ivy pointed out.

"My feet are out because they didn't want your feet to be lonely," Jack said. "My feet are . . . chivalrous."

"Oh, nice," Ivy said. "I like to know that you're always brave and true."

"I am brave and true," Jack agreed. "I'm also loyal." He lowered his mouth so it was close to her ear. "I'll always be loyal to you. Please don't ... worry about that."

"I'm trying not to worry," Ivy said. "It's just ... you were so adamant."

"You were adamant, too."

"I was adamant because you were adamant."

"Oh, whatever," Jack groaned. "Can we just agree, for the moment, that we're done being adamant?"

"I guess," Ivy said, moving to climb off the couch. "I suppose I should make breakfast. We might have a big day in front of us."

Jack tightened his arms around her waist and pulled her back down. "Five more minutes," he said. "This is the day we're going to solve this. I know it. I want five more minutes of ... this ... before I have to face whatever horrors we've got coming our way."

It wasn't much of a hardship, so Ivy relaxed back against him. "Okay. Five more minutes. Then I'm going to make breakfast and you're going to make coffee."

"Deal."

"**ARE** we working in the greenhouse today?" Kelly asked, her eyes wide as they fixed on Ivy an hour later. Ivy was fresh out of the shower, her hair still damp, but she could read the worry on Kelly's face.

"We are," Ivy said. "I thought that being away from everyone – just the two of us – would be a nice way to spend the afternoon."

Kelly was resigned, and yet resolute at the same time. "Okay. Um ... is it all right if I go and get set up in the greenhouse first? You still have a few minutes to get ready, and I want to ... get comfortable."

"I think that's fine," Ivy said, sympathy rolling off of her. "This is really going to be okay, Kelly. I promise."

"I hope you're right," Kelly said. "I just need a few minutes to collect myself. Should I take some bottles of water down?"

"That's a good idea," Ivy said. "I'll be about twenty minutes behind you."

"I'll be waiting."

Once the teenager was gone, Ivy went about her normal morning routine. After drying her hair, she tied it up in a loose ponytail so she wouldn't have to worry about it. She was dressed and almost out the back door when someone knocked on the front door.

Curious, Ivy left the picnic basket she'd packed on the kitchen table and shuffled to the door. The man she found standing there was not who she was expecting. He was … average. He was average height. He had average looks. He even wore nondescript clothing. "Can I help you?"

"I hope so," the man said. "My name is Gil Thorpe. I'm … Kelly Sisto's guidance counselor."

"Oh," Ivy said, realization dawning. "Jack told me he questioned you. He said you were trying to help Kelly. How can I help you?"

"Well, ever since Detective Harker and his partner came to visit me, I haven't been able to get Kelly out of my head," Gil said. "I … can I come in?"

"Of course," Ivy said, pushing the door open and ushering the nervous man inside. "Please, have a seat."

Once they were settled, the look Gil sent Ivy was plaintive. "I know this is none of my business," he said. "I've told myself a hundred times to stay out of it. It's just … I grew rather fond of Kelly. When you're in a position like I am, you know you can't help all of the students.

"Heck, I know I can't help most of the students," he continued. "I just want to be able to help Kelly."

"It sounds like you're good at your job," Ivy said. "It's actually good that you're here. Kelly is ready to tell me what happened to her today. I was just on my way to go to her. You might be able to give me some insight into what to expect."

"Kelly isn't here?" Gil asked, disappointed.

"Not technically," Ivy said. "She's just over at my nursery. You can't see it from here, but it abuts the back of my property. It only takes me five minutes to walk through the woods to get there. So, she's here … but not here … if that makes any sense."

"Ah, I see," Gil said. "You said Kelly was going to open up to you today? Does that mean she's been quiet up until now?"

"She's been pretty tight-lipped," Ivy said. "She's talked about some of her feelings regarding her parents' death, and we reintroduced her to her brother last night."

"Jordan? I had no idea he was still in the area."

"Actually, he's not far away," Ivy said. "He's living over in Gaylord. Once we get Kelly set up in a more permanent home, they're going to schedule regular visitation days and get to know one another again. I think seeing him did her a world of good last night."

"Is that why she's suddenly interested in talking?"

"I think she's always wanted to tell me the truth," Ivy said. "Something keeps stopping her. I think … I think she's ashamed."

"What does she have to be ashamed about?" Gil asked.

"I'm honestly not sure," Ivy said. "Jack mentioned an older boyfriend, and I'm starting to think she kept him a secret for a reason. Maybe he pressured her into doing something illegal. I have no idea if that's the truth, but that's my current theory."

"Kelly never mentioned an older boyfriend to me," Gil said. "I think that's teenage gossip."

"Well, as I'm sure you know, teenage gossip usually gets out of hand," Ivy said. "That doesn't mean it's not true, though. I think Kelly probably did have an older boyfriend. Just because she didn't want to tell you about him, that doesn't mean he's not real.

"You're an adult," she continued. "She might've thought you were going to turn him in. She's only sixteen. Anyone over the age of eighteen spending time with her would automatically be suspect."

Gil bit his lower lip as he glanced around the cottage. "You make a good point," he said. "I was one of the few people Kelly opened up to, though. I honestly think she would've told me."

Ivy held up her hands in a placating manner. The man obviously didn't like being told he wasn't thoroughly doing his job. "I didn't mean to denigrate you in any way," she said. "I just think that teenage girls are a specific … beast. They hide things. Trust me. I was a teenager once."

"I'm sure you were," Gil said. "I was hoping to get a chance to talk to Kelly. Detective Harker told me it would be a possibility."

Jack had never mentioned anything of the sort to Ivy, and without realizing why, her danger alarm started to ding in the back of her head. "Really? He didn't tell me that."

"He thought seeing a familiar face would propel Kelly into telling the truth," Gil said.

"Oh, well, that makes sense," Ivy said, getting to her feet. "I'll just give him a call and make sure it's okay, and then I'll take you over to the greenhouse."

"I'm sure he's busy," Gil said. Even though her back was to him, Ivy could hear the shift in his voice and knew he'd gotten to his feet as well. "There's no need to bother him."

"I'm sure you're right," Ivy said, making her decision quickly. "The greenhouse is easier to get to through the back. Can you grab that picnic basket off the table on your way through? I packed a lunch. There's plenty in there for everyone."

"Will your nursery be busy today?" Gil asked.

"It's generally busy on the weekends," Ivy said, fighting to keep her demeanor calm. "It should be pretty empty today."

"That's good," Gil said.

Ivy moved toward the sliding doors, prepared to bolt through them as soon as she had a clear shot. Once she was in the woods and away from Gil, she was going to call Jack. Whatever secret Kelly was hiding, Ivy was sure it revolved around this man. "We should get going."

"We should," Gil agreed. "In case I haven't mentioned it, I'm glad you upgraded your front door. That wood one you had before wasn't enough to keep an attractive woman like yourself safe."

Ivy's heart plummeted. He wasn't even keeping up the pretense of playing games now. He was putting all of his cards on the table. "I just wish it was a different color," she said, taking another step toward the glass door. If she could make it two more steps she'd be able to run to freedom – and relative safety. No one knew the woods surrounding her house as well as she did.

Ivy had just about convinced herself that salvation was at hand when a figure hopped up onto the patio. It was Kelly. "Oh, no."

"What great timing," Gil said. "I guess we don't have to find Kelly after all."

This couldn't be happening, Ivy thought. This had to be a dream. If only she could call Jack into this nightmare with the power of her mind.

TWENTY-FIVE

"What's taking you so long?" Kelly asked, pushing the glass door open and fixing Ivy with a quizzical look. "I thought you forgot about me."

"Run," Ivy muttered.

"What?"

"Run."

"Don't run," Gil said, drawing Kelly's attention to him.

"Oh, no," Kelly said, her face draining of color. "I … what are you doing here?"

"Looking for you, my love," Gil said.

Ivy's stomach contorted into knots at the term of endearment. She still wasn't sure what was going on, but she had a sickening suspicion … and it was one that made her stomach turn.

"Run, Kelly," Ivy said. "I … . She froze when she heard the unmistakable sound of a gun cocking.

"Don't run, Kelly," Gil said, his voice eerily calm. "If you run, I'm going to kill your little friend here. Is that what you want?"

"No," Kelly said, her mouth dry. "I … please, don't hurt her."

"Everyone needs to come in and sit down," Gil instructed. "Ms.

Morgan, if you would be so kind as to shut that door – and lock it – I'll be so kind as to not put a bullet into the back of your head."

Ivy pressed her eyes shut briefly, but then she did as she was told, making sure the sound of the door locking was loud and evident, even though she knew the door hadn't caught in its proper place. It was a defect in the lock, but there was no way Gil could know about it.

"Everyone should come and take a seat," Gil said. "We all need to have a little talk."

"Gil, don't do this," Kelly begged. "I … I'm sorry I ran. It was a mistake. I shouldn't have done it. You just scared me."

"I didn't mean to scare you," Gil said, his eyes earnest when Ivy turned to stare him down. "You shouldn't have run away from me, though. You've made a mess of this whole situation."

"I know," Kelly said, licking her lips. "I … I can make it better."

"You're going to make it better," Gil said. "Sit down."

Kelly obediently took a spot on the couch, lowering her gaze to her knees and sitting ramrod straight. Ivy recognized the posture for what it was: submission.

"Ms. Morgan, if you would be so kind as to have a seat next to Kelly, I'd really appreciate it," Gil said, waving the gun in Ivy's face for emphasis. Ivy wasn't familiar with handguns. She didn't know makes, models, or calibers, but she was pretty certain Gil was serious – and he knew how to use the weapon in his hand.

Ivy reluctantly moved through the living room and settled on the couch next to Kelly. Her heart was pounding, and her mind was muddled with possible escape scenarios. Unfortunately for her, none of the ones she came up with ended with anything other than death.

Once Ivy was in position, Gil sat back down in the armchair and fixed both women with a bright smile. "Isn't this better? Now we can all have a nice discussion without anyone doing anything stupid."

"I think you've already done something stupid," Ivy said, her voice wavering.

"You don't know what you're talking about," Gil said. "Please refrain from speaking unless someone speaks to you. That's the general rule of life, Ms. Morgan. I'm not here for you today. I'm here for my beloved Kelly."

Ivy shifted her gaze to the shaking teenager, worry clogging her heart.

"Kelly, I have to know, what possessed you to run?" Gil asked. "I thought we were having a perfectly nice evening. I went out of my way to set up a nice evening picnic for us, and when I went back to my car to get another bottle of wine, I found your spot empty. You just left me in the middle of nowhere."

"I was scared," Kelly said, never moving her eyes up to a defiant position. "You were … mean … that night."

"I'm never mean," Gil countered. "I teach important life lessons. You agreed when we started dating that I was in charge."

"Dating?" Ivy couldn't keep her mouth shut. She knew it was a mistake, but she had to take the onus of the conversation off of Kelly. "You're sick. You can't date a teenager. You're an adult. She's a child."

"Oh, she's not a child," Gil said. "She hasn't been a child for quite some time. We have a very special bond, Ms. Morgan. It's one you couldn't possibly understand, or embrace. That's neither here nor there, though. I wasn't talking to you."

"I'm sorry, Gil," Kelly said. "I won't do it again. You can take me. I'll go willingly. Don't hurt Ivy, though. She was just trying to help me."

"She didn't help you, though, did she? She made you forget your place," Gil said. "Where is your place, Kelly?"

"With you." Kelly sounded pathetic, and the more she talked – the more stock answers she graced Gil with – the angrier Ivy got. "I've always belonged with you."

"That's right," Gil said, waving the gun around. "I'm your boyfriend. I'm in charge. I told you what would happen if you ran. I told you what would happen if someone found out about our relationship. Why didn't you listen?"

"I didn't mean to disobey you," Kelly said. "It's just … that whip thing hurts. I told you it hurts. You said you wouldn't use it again, but you did."

"I only use it when you forget your manners," Gil said. "Now look at the mess you've gotten us into. How do you expect us to go back to our happy life now that your friend here knows about our relationship?"

"I ... she won't tell anyone," Kelly said. "She'll promise to keep it quiet, won't you?" Kelly's eyes were pleading when she risked a glance in Ivy's direction.

"No," Ivy said, shifting her attention to Gil. "You're a sick bastard. You used your position of power as a high school guidance counselor to ... groom her. You made her think you were in a relationship when you were just using her for sex. You're going to get locked up for the rest of your life, and I'm going to laugh my ass off when it happens."

Gil backhanded Ivy, his hand lashing out quickly as he smacked her. Hard. Ivy reared back, grabbing her cheek as she cast murderous looks in Gil's direction. "Don't talk back to me," Gil warned. "I can see you haven't been trained properly. I'm looking forward to taking on that task myself."

"I'd rather die."

"That can be arranged," Gil said. "Seriously, Ms. Morgan, how do you expect this to go? I'm the one in charge here. I'm the one with the gun. You're either going to start towing the line or the line is going to tow you."

"Do what he says," Kelly warned. "He'll ... hurt you ... if you don't."

Ivy had no intention of following one order from this man. She also knew she was in a precarious situation. She had to find a way to get Kelly out of the house. She couldn't take on Gil Thorpe when Kelly was in the line of fire.

Ivy was desperate for help, but she knew none was coming. Jack was at work. He was tracking down leads on Kelly's case. He didn't know anything was wrong. Max was at the lumber yard working. He wasn't planning on painting her door until the weekend. Ivy was alone, and she knew it.

Jack! I need you!

. . .

"**HOW** DID things go with Jordan Sisto last night?" Brian asked, moving over to Jack's desk and studying his partner. "You look like you slept well again, by the way. Snuggling up to Ivy must be good for your complexion."

Jack ignored the barb. "Jordan and Kelly had a nice reunion," he said. "I was worried at first, but Kelly didn't even get a chance to be mean to him. The second she saw him she started crying."

"Is she okay?"

"They hugged, and we all had a nice dinner," Jack said. "Jordan pushed her to tell the truth last night, and Kelly said she needed a little more time. I have a feeling she and Ivy are having a long discussion right now."

"Will Ivy call when she knows what's going on?"

"That's what she promised," Jack said. "Do you have any leads on a new foster home for Kelly?"

"I have a few," Brian said. "I was kind of hoping we could keep her in town. Maggie Lawson takes in foster kids, and her house is empty right now. She's a good woman. She's strong, but fair. I'm going to go out and talk to her this afternoon."

"That's good," Jack said, focusing on his computer screen.

"What are you looking at?" Brian asked.

"Kelly's school records."

"We've already looked," Brian said. "There's nothing there."

"I know," Jack said. "It's just … I have this feeling we're missing something."

"Of course we're missing something," Brian said. "We have a teenager who was found hiding in a greenhouse. She had bruises all over her arms. She won't tell us what happened to her. We're missing something pretty big."

Jack made a face. "Thank you, Mr. Obvious."

Brian's face softened. "What do you think we're missing?"

"I don't know," Jack said. "There's something odd here, though. Didn't that guidance counselor … what was his name, Gil Thorpe?"

Brian nodded.

"Did he tell us Kelly only did enough to get by in school?"

"Yeah," Brian said. "He said she was really smart, but since no one challenged her, she put in minimal effort so she wouldn't get in trouble."

"That's not what these records show," Jack said.

"What do they show?"

"Up until the spring semester – this past semester – she was getting straight As," Jack said. "Her whole transcript shows all As ... except for a B in gym class two years ago. Her record is perfect until this most recent semester."

"And what does that semester show?"

"All Cs and below," Jack said.

"Kids don't just fall off the rails like that," Brian said, rubbing the back of his neck. "They're usually pretty consistent unless something shoves them off the rails."

"Exactly," Jack said. "Something happened in the last six months to shove Kelly off the rails."

"What do you think it was? Is this where the older boyfriend comes into play?"

"Maybe," Jack conceded. "What if the older boyfriend is even older than we think?"

"Meaning?"

"What if an adult started preying on Kelly?" Jack suggested. "What if the older boyfriend was really someone in a position of power over Kelly?"

"You think an adult is having sex with her and using her for ... something horrible, don't you?"

"I think it's a possibility," Jack said. "We both know sexual abuse is one of the things that can toss a kid off the rails."

"Do you think it was the foster father?"

"No," Jack said. "Don't get me wrong, that guy is a jerkwad. Kelly wasn't spending very many nights in their house, though. A predator wants access to his prey as much as possible. If it was Gideon, he would've forced Kelly under his roof seven nights a week."

"I guess that makes sense," Brian said, rubbing his chin thoughtfully. "Kelly didn't have access to a lot of adults. Although, to be fair, we have no idea where she was spending her nights."

"I think … ." Jack broke off, unsure he wanted to give voice to the suspicion rolling through his brain.

"Tell me," Brian prodded.

"Why did the counselor lie about her grades? Why did he tell us she was a liar? He was laying the groundwork for us to disbelieve her. Why?"

"You think it's him?" Brian asked, flabbergasted. "But … why?"

"Most guidance counselors and teachers are good people," Jack said. "Predators try to infiltrate schools, though. Then they pick the most at-risk kids to … groom."

"The counselor would've known that Kelly was getting good grades until the most recent semester and he didn't let on," Brian said.

"He lied to us," Jack said. "Not only that, but he tried to make us think what he wanted us to believe."

"That still doesn't explain how Kelly ended up in Shadow Lake."

"It doesn't," Jack agreed. "It gives us a place to focus, though."

"Shouldn't we wait until Kelly tells us what happened?"

"I'm tired of waiting," Jack said. "The counselor being the one to abuse Kelly makes sense. She's scared to tell us what happened in case we can't protect her. People have fallen down on the job when it comes to protecting her for eight years."

"What do you want to do?"

"I … ." Jack broke off, a whisper rippling across his skin. It was almost as if he could hear Ivy's voice. *Jack! I need you!*

Jack jumped to his feet, his heart racing.

"What's wrong?" Brian asked, surprised.

"I don't know," Jack said. "I … we need to get out to Ivy's house."

"Why?"

"It's just a feeling," Jack said. "Something is wrong."

"How can you be sure?"

"I can't," Jack said, grabbing his keys. "I'd rather be wrong and look like an idiot than be right and do nothing, though. Come on."

TWENTY-SIX

"How long has he been abusing you, Kelly?" Ivy asked, her gaze never moving from Gil's face.

"I am not an abuser," Gil said.

"You're nothing but an abuser," Ivy countered. "You put yourself in a position of power, and then you watched … and waited. You were looking for a student to fit your specific needs. You needed someone who didn't have overzealous parents. You needed someone who you thought the system had overlooked. That's how you found Kelly."

"Shut up," Gil seethed. "You have no idea what you're talking about."

"I know exactly what I'm talking about," Ivy snapped. "You're a monster. You convinced Kelly that you loved her, because you knew that was the one thing she was most desperate for in her life.

"How did it start? Did you ply her with compliments? Did you tell her she was special? Did you isolate her from any friends she might possibly have?" Ivy asked.

"We're in love," Gil said. "Once Kelly is of legal age, we're going to get married."

"And then you can abuse her to your heart's content, right? You make me sick."

"You have no idea the depth of the love Kelly and I share," Gil countered. "We're soul mates."

"Soul mates don't hurt one another," Ivy argued. "Soul mates don't beat someone. They don't leave bruises on someone. They don't take them out into a field for a picnic and do … God knows whatever you had planned for her that night."

"He beat me all the time," Kelly said, her voice small. "The first time it happened, he apologized. He said it was an accident. I thought he really loved me."

"No one blames you," Ivy said. "He manipulated you."

"I knew what he was doing was wrong," Kelly said. "It's my fault. I could've gotten away before it got out of hand. I was too scared, though. I was too … needy. I wanted to believe he really loved me."

"I do love you," Gil said. "I've loved you from the moment I laid eyes on you."

"How long have you been at her school?" Ivy asked.

"What does that matter?" Gil was starting to get angry. "Love is love."

"He didn't start until this past year," Kelly said.

"How long was it before he started having special meetings with you?"

"A couple of months," Kelly said.

"How long before he started having sex with you?"

"We spent Christmas together," Kelly said, her shoulders shaking as she started to sob. "He bought me a necklace and told me he loved me. Then he gave me some wine. Before that, I would just go to his house to talk. I swear. I … still don't know how it happened that first time."

"I do," Ivy said, glaring at Gil. "He groomed you with words, and he made it so you were comfortable coming to his house. Then he got your inhibitions down with the wine. I'm betting the first few times he gave you wine he didn't touch you, did he?"

Kelly shook her head, her tears falling freely now.

"He wanted to make sure you thought everything he was doing was above board," Ivy said. "He wanted to convince you that he was a good guy. I'm betting, once Jack looks into his background, we're going to find a lot of vulnerable girls in his wake. That's just how he operates. You can't blame yourself."

"I should've told someone," Kelly said. "I should've told you. I'm so sorry."

"I know you are," Ivy said. "Don't worry about it. I knew something horrible happened to you. I had no idea it was this horrible, but that first day – when you screamed because men tried to touch you – I knew. I tried to convince myself I was wrong, though.

"I didn't want anything this bad to have happened to you," she continued. "I made the mistake. I let myself believe something else was going on. You didn't do anything wrong, Kelly. No matter what happens, you have to believe that."

"Are you done?" Gil asked, rolling his eyes. "Good grief. You like to hear yourself talk, don't you?"

"I don't care what you do to me," Ivy said. "You're not touching that girl again, though. I won't stand for it."

"How do you think you're going to stop me?"

"Any way I have to," Ivy said.

Gil chuckled hoarsely. "Let me tell you a little bit about yourself that you probably don't already know, Ms. Morgan," he said. "You fancy yourself as a crusader. You're going to right all the wrongs in the world. You only have one way of looking at the world: your way.

"You don't care if you have a narrow belief system, and you don't care if others have viable ways of living their lives," he continued. "You've decided what's right and wrong in this world, and there's nothing that's going to change your mind. You're the problem here, not the solution."

Ivy scorched him with a look. "Is that what you really think?"

Gil nodded.

"Well then, let me tell you a little bit about yourself that you probably don't already know," Ivy spat. "You look at life like someone owes you something. You walk around with your chest puffed out and think the world has done you wrong.

"You're not handsome, and yet you think you are," she continued.

"You think people overlook your features because there's something wrong with them, not you. It's always someone else who makes the mistake. It's never you. Do you know what that's the definition for? Insanity.

"You can't interact with people your own age because you're a narcissist," Ivy said. "I don't know if you were always sexually attracted to teenagers, but you realized a long time ago they were the only ones who would be willing to let you mold them. Real women – adult women – saw through you. You freaked them out. You disgusted them.

"That's when you decided to move on to teenagers," she continued. "I don't know who your first was, but Kelly clearly wasn't it. I'm sure you've got a spotty record, and instead of calling attention to themselves, various school officials quietly cut you loose instead of reporting you to the cops. That's on them, and they're just as guilty as you are.

"I don't know what your endgame is here, but I can tell you it's not going to play out how you think it is," Ivy said. "Jack is going to figure out what you've done, and God help you when he comes for you."

"Jack isn't smart enough to find his own ass with both of his hands," Gil said. "He sat in my living room and let me lead him to answers that weren't even true. So much for your beloved hero."

Ivy ignored the dig. "He'll come for you," she said. "He'll kill you."

"Is that because he's in love with you?" Gil asked. "I couldn't help but notice that he's been staying here the past few nights. He's made it impossible to reclaim my love during the evening, which is why I had to approach you when he was at work. How smart was that? He left you alone and vulnerable."

"Please, don't hurt her," Kelly whimpered. "I'll go with you. I won't run away again. I'll … let you do whatever you want to me. Just … don't hurt Ivy."

"You're not going anywhere with him," Ivy said. "He's never touching you again."

"Oh, you're awfully sure of yourself," Gil sneered. "Have you forgotten that I'm the one with the gun? I think you have." He reached over and grabby Ivy by the back of her hair, gripping her ponytail and yanking her to her feet. He shook her viciously, and then pressed the gun to her chin. "Who is in charge now, you bitch?"

"I'M GOING TO KILL HIM," Jack snarled. "I'm going to … ."

"Calm down," Brian whispered, elevating himself slightly so he could look through Ivy's window without calling attention to himself. "We need to make a plan here. Ivy is pushing him to focus his anger on her. She's trying to protect Kelly."

"She's going to protect Kelly by sacrificing herself," Jack said, his voice cracking. "I … I'll kill him."

"We can't wait for more backup," Brian said, forcing his voice to remain even. "What do you want to do?"

Jack rubbed the back of his neck, his back pressed to the side of Ivy's small cottage as he hunkered down. He scanned the front yard, helplessness washing over him, and then his eyes landed on the metal bistro table on the porch. "I have an idea."

"I can't wait to hear this," Brian said.

"You're going to go to the back patio," Jack said, his voice eerily calm. "I'm going to throw that table through the front window and follow it inside. While I'm grappling with Thorpe, you're going to go in through the back and get them out."

"What happens if Thorpe shoots you?" Brian asked.

"It won't be the first time."

"I know that," Brian said. "I know all about your history. I'm not just going to stand by and let you get shot. There has to be another way."

"I won't risk Ivy," Jack said. "I can't."

"You're in love with her, aren't you?"

Jack didn't answer the question. He didn't know how to. He couldn't put a name to his feelings for Ivy because he wasn't sure what they were. The only thing he knew with absolute clarity was that he wouldn't fail her. She'd saved him in his dreams, helping him put his past behind him. Now he was going to save her in reality, and hopefully ensure a future he didn't even know he wanted until recently. "I won't let her die," Jack said, his voice grim. "Go to the back. Ivy and Kelly are your priority. Don't worry about me."

"You and I are going to have a long talk when this is over with," Brian warned, but he did as Jack asked.

Jack gave Brian a few minutes to get into position, and then he scampered to the front porch on his hands and knees. He gripped the small table with both hands and heaved with all his might, tossing the table through the window and shattering the glass into a million pieces.

IT WAS like an explosion inside of the house, and even though she was terrified, Ivy kept her wits about her and jerked away from Gil. Jack was here. She knew it, and more importantly, she felt it. She dropped to her knees, grabbing Kelly by the hand and directing her to the other side of the couch.

"Crawl," Ivy hissed.

Kelly instinctively followed Ivy's directions, cringing when the woman sheltered Kelly's body with her own.

"What the hell?" Gil asked, turning his attention to the front window. "I … what … ?"

Jack launched himself through the front window, his hands empty of a weapon as he landed on Gil. His fists were furious as they rained punches down on the guidance counselor, and Jack used his left hand to wrestle the gun toward the ceiling. He was taller than Gil, and he was definitely stronger. He hit him one more time, toppling him to the floor, and then he confiscated the gun.

"Wow," Brian said, appearing in the archway between the kitchen and living room. "You didn't even give me a chance to get into position."

"I waited as long as I could," Jack said, gasping for breath. He handed the gun wordlessly to Brian. "Cuff this piece of … filth." He kicked the prone man in the ribs for good measure, an act Brian conveniently opted to ignore.

Jack pushed his way around the couch, his gaze falling on Kelly as she cowered in the corner. He dropped to his knees, surprised to find tears running down his face. He'd survived. He wasn't sure when he jumped through the window if that was possible. All he cared about was Ivy and Kelly making it.

Ivy lifted her hand, her fingertips moving through his tears as she cupped his cheek. "How did you know?"

"I heard you call for me," Jack said.

"I called for you in my mind."

"No," Jack said, shaking his head. "You called to me with your heart."

Jack reached for Ivy and hugged her tightly, only releasing her so she could pull Kelly close. He settled on the ground with both of them, wrapping his arms around a fragile teenage girl – and the woman who was willing to die for her – and letting them cry until they couldn't wring out another tear.

It was over. Finally.

TWENTY-SEVEN

Ivy opened the door the next night to find Jack standing on her porch, a simple purple rose in his hand as he extended it in her direction.

Ivy took the bloom wordlessly, pressing it to her nose and inhaling deeply.

Jack watched her, using every ounce of energy he had not to focus on the dark bruise that marred her perfect cheek. "How are you today, honey?"

"I haven't seen you since this morning," Ivy said, lifting her eyes to his. "I thought you … forgot about me."

"That's not possible," Jack said. He extended his hand. "Let's take a walk."

"Another walk?"

"It's time to talk," Jack said. "In fact, we have a few things to talk about."

Ivy took his hand without argument, closing her front door and letting him lead her toward the familiar trees. "Are you going to tell me what happened with Thorpe?"

After taking the guidance counselor into custody the previous afternoon, Brian and Jack transported him down to the station for booking. Max and Michael arrived not long after, and because Max was a guy who knew people in the construction business, they had the window fixed before nightfall.

Kelly was a mess, and she spent hours opening up to Ivy about her ordeal with Gil Thorpe. Ivy had figured out most of the details on her own, but she'd let the girl talk until she couldn't manage to find more words. Then she'd plied her with soup and tucked her into bed.

Jack returned to Ivy's house shortly before ten, too tired to chat for a long period of time. Instead, he'd pulled her down on the couch, tucked her in at his side, and fell into a dreamless sleep. Ivy and Jack didn't visit each other that night, but they also didn't stray far from one another. Jack's arms were tight around her small frame for eight hours straight. Neither of them moved, and when morning beckoned, Jack kissed her and said he had a few things to deal with before they could talk.

That was twelve hours ago.

In that time, Brian arrived at her house with a court order relinquishing Kelly to her brother's care. He'd pulled a few strings – and even though Kelly was happy for Ivy's support, she was ready to move to a permanent spot with her brother. She wanted a family of her own, and she was finally going to get it. Jordan thanked Ivy profusely and promised once Kelly was settled, they would figure out a regular visitation schedule for Ivy – one that included a summer job at the nursery.

With tears in her eyes, Ivy said goodbye to Kelly and wished her a wonderful life. She was just happy she was going to be around to see it.

After that, Ivy waited for Jack to return. And waited. And waited. She'd almost given up when the knock came.

"Thorpe has admitted everything," Jack said. "He's going for an insanity defense, though. He said he has urges he can't control, and he never coerced Kelly into doing anything."

"That won't hold up in court, will it?"

"Nope," Jack said. "Don't worry. Gil Thorpe is going away for life."

"That's good," Ivy said. "Did you know Jordan was going to get custody of Kelly?"

"I was hopeful," Jack said. "We put the paperwork in yesterday. Because of his unblemished record, and the fact that his boss showed up to say he would have help, the judge agreed Kelly should be with her family.

"She's going to have regular visits from a social worker, and the court is recommending family therapy for both Jordan and Kelly, but Jordan is open to all of it," Jack said. "I think Kelly is finally going to get what she's always wanted."

"You didn't get a chance to say goodbye, though."

"There is no goodbye, honey," Jack said. "I heard she's going to come and work for you in a few weeks. I'll see her then."

"Are you going to be spending a lot of time at the nursery?" Ivy asked, readying herself for the second part of their talk.

"I'm going to be spending a lot of time around you," Jack said.

"Are you sure?"

Jack led her through the woods, not answering – or stopping – until he was in front of her fairy ring. Ivy's heart flopped when she saw the blanket, complete with a picnic basket, sitting in the middle of the ring. "Oh, wow."

"Don't worry, I made sure there was no Poison Ivy around," Jack teased.

"I … I don't want to do this if you're going to break my heart, Jack," Ivy said. "I can't take it."

"I have no intention of breaking your heart," Jack said. "I can't make promises about forever. Not yet, at least. I can promise you that I've never wanted anything as much as I want you."

He glanced down at Ivy, rubbing her unblemished cheek with his thumb. "I'm not going to fight this any longer," he said. "It hurts too much to be away from you. I want to have a chance with you. I want us to have a chance together. I need to know if that's what you want, too."

"I've been drawn to you from that first moment I saw you," Ivy said, her lower lip quivering. "I want you, but I'm scared."

"I know," Jack said. "I'm scared, too. Maybe it's time that we're scared together instead of apart."

"You know people are going to always whisper about me in town, right? You know I'm not normal."

"I've always known you're not normal," Jack said, tilting her chin up. "I'm not normal either. I think we're going to be happy if we both agree to be odd together."

"Do you want to be happy?"

It was a pointed question, and Jack was ready for it. "I didn't think I could ever be happy again after … what happened. I didn't think I'd ever want to share that with anyone. I was wrong, on both counts. You make me happy. You make me smile. You make me laugh.

"My heart sings when you're around," he continued. "I always want to touch you. I'm tired of fighting those instincts. I want to be with you. I want to make you happy. I can't do it all on my own, though. You're going to have to meet me in the middle."

"I want to be with you, too," Ivy said, a tear slipping down her cheek. "I want to touch you."

Jack smiled. "Then let's start now," he said, lowering his lips to hers.

The kiss was soft, neediness put aside for another night. Jack tugged Ivy into his arms and held her close, rubbing her back as he lifted her. When they parted, Ivy's face was practically glowing.

"Does this mean I get to pick where we dream tonight?"

"Yes," Jack said. "If you make me pick vegetables, though, I'm breaking up with you."

Ivy laughed, the sound warming Jack's heart. "I have a fun place for us to visit."

"Let's finish enjoying this place first," Jack prodded. "We've got a lot of nights in front of us. We don't have to pick one destination yet. We have forever, and everywhere."

Ivy kissed him again. This time it was slow and sensuous, the promise of forever on her lips and in her heart. Jack gave in and accepted everything she had to offer, and Ivy did the same.

There was no turning back now.

Made in United States
Orlando, FL
23 December 2023

41611459R00125